AF439869

MARY'S

REVENGE

Mary McCaferty
Born July 22 1980

THE AUTHOR

Jack Anderson

Please note that the names of the
characters in this book are all fictitious.

The similarity to any persons living
or dead is pure coincidence.

All the Towns, City's and Police
Stations in Scotland
are real places,

The street names, bars, and
shops are fictitious.

The four stars Hotel El Puntazo II in Mojacar,
Spain, and the Craws Nest Hotel in Pittem-
weem, Scotland are real establishments.

MY LAST TWO NOVELS

'The Barrylairg Mystery'

And
'Fear in her Eyes'

Friends, who had read my last two books, had mentioned to me about the character of Mary McCaferty,

"She was a bit of a bitch. Why don't you
write a book on her?" they said,

Well why not, I thought, so here it is. For
those readers who have not read my previous
books, Mary always seemed to be attracted to
trouble. However, she always managed to take
matters into her own hands and get revenge.
God help anyone who crossed her.
Do not mess with a McCaferty
was her favourite saying.

A SPECIAL MENTION
MUST GO TO SHEILA.

The amount of times I had ignored her
speaking to me, because of the concentration
I had during my time writing this book,
she has been extremely patient with me.

Jack and Sheila Anderson

CHAPTER 1

The early years.

Sean McCaferty, Mary's father, worked with a Ship-building Company in Cork, Southern Ireland. Mary was three months old and her brother Gerry, three years old, when the family moved to Fife, Scotland in 1980. He applied for a job with RGC Offshore Methil. This was when the oilrig boom was on, and Sean was wanting in at the beginning. With his engineering skills, he would receive a much larger salary than he did in Ireland.

He, along with his wife Margaret, son Gerry, and daughter Mary moved into a home in Kirkcaldy, Fife, which is only a few miles along the Fife coast from Methil.

Both Gerry and Mary had red hair and as a result, they were often called names like, copper top and Ginger. Gerry quickly put these boys in their place with a punch on the nose.

At five years old, when Mary started school, she had very long red hair and many freckles. When boys shouted names at her, Gerry was always there to care for his little sister; he would take them aside and threaten to smash their faces in.

Gerry soon earned a reputation not to be messed with, and he taught Mary how to take care of herself so that she would not be messed with either.

Mary's early years saw her being a bit of a tomboy; however, that would change when she neared her teen years.

At twelve years of age, she realised that there was big changes beginning with her body. She had been listening to the other girls in her class and knew that it meant periods.

Unfortunately, Mary felt embarrassed about it and did not inform her mum, and she struggled to begin with. One day, Fay Anderson her teacher at school, noticed that Mary was upset about something and she asked her to remain behind class, "What have I done miss?" she asked, and the teacher replied, "Nothing Mary, I just want to ask you something." After class, the teacher told Mary that she knew there was something wrong, she had noticed that Mary was not the happy girl she had been, and that she always needed to go to the bathroom. Mary explained that she had started her periods and she was not to sure how to deal with them, that was the reason she was always going to the bathroom.

Fay Anderson put her arm round Mary and asker her why she had not told her mum. Mary told her about being too embarrassed.

Fay told her that she would help her. She said that

she would take her home with her, and she would explain what she was required to do. While they were at Fay's home, she explained everything to Mary, and told her that every female had this to go through, it was part of life for all females, so there was nothing to be embarrassed about.

She also said to Mary that she would have a quiet word with her mum. Mary thanked her and said that she appreciated it. As the weeks passed, Fay could see a vast improvement in Mary, she was back to her self-confident best.

By the time Mary was fourteen she had lost nearly all of the freckles, and she was a very beautiful young girl, she looked more as if she was seventeen years old.

The older boys were now paying her much more attention, and Gerry knew what they were after. They were well warned, even though he knew that his little sister could fend for herself.

In 1994, Margaret McCaferty, Mary and Gerry's mother, died of cancer. Only a few months before her death, she had eventually announced to the family, that she had been diagnosed with cancer, and it had come as a very sudden shock to the family. Margaret had not been feeling well for a long time, but she had kept it to herself; she had always been that kind of a person perhaps that was why Mary had been like that as well.

From being a happy family, to loosing a wife and mother in only such a short time, had hit them very hard. Fourteen-year-old Mary was devastated with the loss of her mother and Gerry did his best to comfort her, he could see the reaction that his father had with his wife's death, and the effect it was having on him.

Sean had begun drinking a lot; however, thankfully, he had the sense to be sober enough to continue his work. At fourteen, Mary had taken on the roll of becoming the mother in the house.

Two years later in 1996, Sean McCaferty was seriously injured in a vehicle accident. It happened one cold frosty January morning, while on his way to work in Methil. His car had skidded on the icy road surface and veered into the wrong lane, he hit a cement mixer truck head on. Sean never fully recovered from his injuries, and he died three months later.

Another devastating occurrence to the family, and Mary was wondering what she and Gerry would do next. With the major money earner now gone, they could not afford the rent of the three-bedroom council home. Even with Gerry's' pay packet they could not afford the payments.

They had no option but to leave their family home, however with his driving job, and the wage he earned, Gerry managed to rent a one bedroom flat in Kirkcaldy.

Mary, who by now had left school, moved in with her brother and she had begun a job as a trainee hairdresser and beautician. With the small wage she earned, she was only able to contribute a little to the rent, so she had to sleep on the couch, which was not the ideal lifestyle for a sixteen-year-old girl.

Every now and again, she had a little cry on the shoulder of her brother; and he was always there to comfort her.

She would always curse the cancer that took her mother from her, she missed her so much.

The boys were beginning to queue up to take her out, however she coped easily with their advances, especially as she had joined a self-defense class.

One lad, who had thought that he would try his luck with her, soon found out that she was no pushover. Mary grabbed the lad's hand, which was slowly moving up under her blouse, she twisted his arm behind his back then kicked his legs from behind. Now on his knees, Mary was standing behind him with two of her fingers pressing on the lad's eyes. He was begging Mary to let him go; and as she did, she told him that in future he would know not to mess with a McCaferty again.

That message soon got round the rest of her admirers and she had no more trouble from them. When Gerry found out what had happened, he laughed and told her. "Well-done lass, you keep telling them that."

CHAPTER 2

Who used the knife?

Mary, Gerry or the victim himself.

After a few months, Mary who had now just turned seventeen, was walking home one night from one of her classes, she was passing a lane, when a masked man jumped out from it and held a knife to her neck. As he pulled her into the lane, he told her not to scream or he would stab her, she pleaded with him, saying that she was only sixteen.

She said, "Please don't rape me, I'm too young, but if you promise not to hurt me I will go down on my knees and satisfy you."

The attacker was taken a little by surprise, but said, "Okay, but remember I have a knife in my hand."

Mary began to loosen his belt and unzip his trousers, and then she knelt down on one knee and pulled the trousers and under pants down round his ankles. She took hold of his penis with one hand and with the other, not noticed by the assailant, she began to fasten his belt.

Within a minute, Mary noticed that the assailant's mind was more on what she was doing, and he had relaxed the arm holding the knife.

She then grabbed his testicles and squeezed hard as she could. As his legs buckled with the pain, Mary sprang to her feet and made off as fast as her legs would take her. As she was running away, she heard the man shout, "You fucking bit… Aaah."

The fact that he had forgotten his pants were now round his ankles and with the belt tightened a little, he could not run; there was a clatter as he fell flat on his face.

When Mary got back to Gerry's flat, he noticed that she was out of breath, and asked her what was wrong. She quickly explained to him what had happened and as she was calling the police, Gerry told her that he was going to go after the man. Because she was now talking on the telephone to the emergency services, she could not stop him.

When he arrived at the Lane he found the man lying in a pool of blood, and he said to himself, "Fucking hell Mary, what did you do to him." Gerry obviously presumed that his sister had lied to him, and that she had stabbed the man, he was thinking that she could be accused with attempted murder, and that he did not want to be involved, so he decided not to hang around. As he was about to leave the scene and head back to his flat to confront his sister, a police car pulled up, and the officers shouted for him to stop.

Gerry did think about making a run for it, and

then changed his mind; after all, he had done nothing. While one officer held on to Gerry's arm the other one took one look at the body lying there, he noticed that the victim was still breathing so he immediately called for an ambulance.

Gerry was immediately handcuffed and cautioned. Even though he protested his innocence, one of the officers told him that as he was about to run from the scene, he had certainly looked very suspicious.

About the same time as Gerry was being cautioned, another two police officers, one of whom was a female officer, were visiting Mary at Gerry's flat, in Denton Road, Kirkcaldy.

After hearing her story, they radioed the officers at the scene and they confirmed that a male had been stabbed and seriously injured.

The WPC told Mary that a man had appeared to have attacked her assailant, and that he had seriously injured him. They also said that they had arrested the man in connection with the assault.

At that, Mary said, "oh god I hope that it's not my brother."

"Why do you say that Ms McCaferty, did you send him there to attack the man who assaulted you?"

Mary said, "No I did not, but it looks like he has done it, doesn't it?"

The officer then cautioned Mary and told her that she would have to go to the police station with them.

"But that man attacked me, why should I get arrested, I'm completely innocent in all this?"
The officer replied, "We shall see what happens after we get you to the station, but in the meantime, as you have been cautioned, I suggest that you do not say anything that may be used against you in court."

On arrival at police headquarters St Brycedale Road, Kirkcaldy, Sergeant Bill Taylor instructed the officers to escort Ms McCaferty to interview room number 2, and that he would see her after talking to Gerry. Mary asked if she could speak to him but she was refused, and told that, it all depended on the outcome of the attack.

In interview room number 1, Inspector Jim Scappa was questioning Gerry and he was not giving him much information. In Gerry's mind, he was sure that Mary had attacked and injured the man who had assaulted her, and he did not want to say anything until he talked to a lawyer.

Inspector Scappa told him that they had his sister in another room and that she had been cautioned as well, he said that it certainly looked like she had put him up to the attack.

"No comment," was Gerry's reply.
The Inspector walked out and into room #2, where he began his questioning of Mary, who also asked for a lawyer. Inspector Scappa tried to explain that it was certainly looking like she had put her brother up to going after the victim and if that was

the case she would be an accomplice to attempted murder.

"No! I did nothing," she shouted.

The inspector told her that her remark would be noted.

Later, after the lawyer had visited the police station and talked to the two of them, he requested that he needed to talk with the Inspector. It was agreed that Gerry was to be remanded in custody for further enquiries, and Mary was to be released on Bail.

A few hours later, it was revealed by the hospital, that the knife had gone into the victim at an angle and that it had not pierced any vital organs, the man had been very lucky. In addition, he would make a good recovery in hospital.

When Ben Clark, the injured man, had recovered enough to talk to the police, and during their questioning, he was trying to think of answers to their questions.

As he had not known about another man being involved, and he did not want to be accused of attacking a woman, he said that he knew nothing of a female being assaulted and that he had been very drunk. "I must have tripped and fell onto the knife. My belt must have come loose and that was how my trousers fell down," he continued, "that was obviously why I tripped."

The next day, after finding out about a man that had been involved, he began to think about what had happened, and then he changed his statement.

It read,

 A woman and a man had jumped out in front of me and as they attacked me with a knife, he demanded money. They probably thought it would be easy as I was drunk. I tried to struggle with them and that was when one of them stabbed me. My belt was loose, and when I tried to move I fell down.

Two police officers went back to the hospital to question Ben Clark again, and when they asked him about his trousers and underpants round his ankles, he said just before the two came at him he had loosened his belt and he was going to have a pee in the darkness of the lane. They fell down as I tried to struggle, and that was how I fell down.

His excuse caused at little bit of amusement from one of the police officers and he said that he might charge him with causing a public nuisance for having a pee in the lane.

Ben shouted back, "with the shock of being stabbed, the urge had gone away, I didnae dae anything so I cannae be charged."

The officer said to the victim that he would report his answers to the inspector at the station and that he would be leaving a constable at the hospital to stop him from leaving.

Next day the report came in from the forensic expert, who had attended the scene, he stated that with the evidence he had obtained from the

Doctor at hospital, and with the evidence from the scene, Ben Clark, the stabbing victim was the guilty party. He stated that the set of fingerprints on the weapon belonged to the victim himself.
None matched with Gerry or Mary McCaferty's prints. He concluded that the statements from Gerry and Mary McCaferty were true. She had disabled him by pulling his pants down and squeezing his testicles. When she had made a run for it, he had tried to catch Ms McCaferty, but then he had tripped up on his pants and stabbed himself as he landed. He continued, according to the doctors at the hospital, the knife had gone into him at an angle, and that it had not pierced any vital organs. They said that the victim had been very lucky, if someone had thrust a knife at the him, and had stabbed it straight in, it would have been more serious and possibly fatal.

In the forensic experts' opinion, the McCaferty's, Gerry and Mary, were innocent and should be cleared of all charges.
Inspector Jim Scappa sent the order through to the prison that Gerry McCaferty should be released immediately.

Two days later, when he was released from hospital, Ben Clark, the victim, was arrested and charged with sexually assaulting Ms Mary McCaferty, also with attempting to pervert the course of justice.

In court, a couple of months later, he received

eighteen months for the attack on Ms McCaferty, and six months for lying to the police.

As he left the court, Ben Clark shouted over to Mary that she would regret what she had done to him. I will get you for this.

CHAPTER 3

The teen years.

By the time Mary was eighteen, it was now just over a year since her experience with the man who had threatened her. She had had some sexual experience with a couple of boy friends but never had full sex with them.

She began thinking that it was about time she lost her virginity, and she decided to take advantage of her popularity. If she started going out with slightly older men, she thought that maybe she could stay the night with them. Which meant that she would have a bed to sleep in instead of the couch at Gerry's flat.

Twenty-year-old Johnny Franks was the one she picked to be her first; he was good looking and had his own little flat, so she hoped that she could spend the night with him. Maybe soon she could be able to move in with him.

Johnny was pleased to have this beauty sharing his bed, and within a couple of days, he did suggest that she stay. However, he told her, as social security paid most of his rent for him, she had to be careful and not let them find out that she lived there as well.

This worked well for about ten months, but Johnny eventually had to tell her that he had been questioned by the social security about a rumour that there were two people living in the flat, so Mary had to leave, and leave right away.

He had denied to them that there was anyone else living there, but of course, it still meant that Mary had to go; he could not take the chance.

Mary now had to find somewhere quickly as she did not fancy more nights on Gerry's couch, especially as he now had a woman living with him.
She began asking all her friends if they knew of anyone with a spare room.

CHAPTER 4

Three Students.

One of Mary's work mates had mentioned it to a few student friends she knew, and one, a man, had offered to sneak her into his place.
When she contacted the man he offered to sneak her into the accommodation; this was on the condition that she may have to take it in turns to share his bed, and with the two other students that lived there.

As she had nowhere else to go, she decided to take them up on their offer, at least on a temporary basis. This was not the kind of arrangement that she wanted, but it was a roof over her head, especially as it was mid winter in Scotland and very cold.

Mary suggested to the three men that she took it in turns to share their beds on a weekly basis; she was thinking that possibly if she could quickly find another place to live, she would only have to spend time with one of them.

The lads, Liam, Noah and Oliver, readily agreed and they even tossed a coin to see who would be first to have her in his bed. That privilege fell to Oliver, who turned out to be a bit shy.

He announced to Mary that he was still a virgin, but pleaded with her not to tell the other two lads.

Mary took this admission to her advantage; she told him that she would say nothing, on the condition that they only had sex once in the week that she slept with him. Oliver readily agreed, as inside he was not even sure if he could do it more than once.

On the fifth night of her living with them, the three men had been out drinking and partying, as they were walking home quite drunk, Oliver, who had been sleeping with Mary, had been bragging to his mates about how good she was in bed. He told them that they had sex every night, and this made his mates very jealous of him. Little did they know it was a lie, he had had sex only the once.

Liam and Noah began suggesting that they both should have sex with her as soon as they get back home; however, Oliver said, "Let's all do it with her at the same time."

Without them even consulting Mary, it was agreed by all three.

When they had eventually staggered back to their flat, it was past midnight, and they could not wait to tell Mary what they were going to do.

As much as she protested, and told them she did not want to, they said, do it or get out.

As it was just after twelve thirty on a freezing cold winter's night, she did not have much option but to comply with them. It was that, or she spent a freezing cold night on the street.

Mary quickly recognised that they were already drunk, and she had an idea to sort them out, she said to them that if they continued their partying, she would strip and dance in front of them while serving them beer.

They all cheered and told her to get her clothes off and get the drink. Every time she went over to them, as she served the drinks, the men had their hands touching her body and squeezing her tits. There was much laughter; Mary, even though she hated what they were doing to her, kept serving them with more drink.

Soon they wanted sex, so to delay them longer, she suggested that they all go naked, and that she would have a little play with their privates, every time she gave them a drink. "The more you drink the more I play with you," she told them.

This brought more cheering, they loved the idea that she would be touching them every time she took them a drink. The beer started to flow even quicker than ever, as each one wanted her to play with him more that the other two.

Little did they realise that Mary had set about getting the men far too drunk to do anything. By about two in the morning, not one of them was able to raise an erection, never mind have sex, even if he had wanted to.

Liam fell asleep about two thirty, and soon after him, Noah did as well. The last one, Oliver, just happened to be the one she had been sleeping with, and she said to him that they have one more drink, and then after he finished it they go right to bed.

With that thought in his mind, he swallowed the drink very quickly and then said, "Shokay let'sh go now."

Mary helped the naked Oliver stagger into his bedroom and into his bed, within seconds of his head hitting the pillow he fell asleep.

Mary collected her belongings and spent the rest of that night alone in Noah's bed.

In the morning, she rose at five thirty, and stepping around the couple of still sleeping drunken men in the living room, she left the apartment and set out on her search for another home. There was no way she was going to live with them any longer. As she walked away, she was swearing to herself that she would get them back one day. They will regret messing with a McCaferty.

CHAPTER 5

Tom Bates.

While she was on her way back to her brothers flat, she met a friend and stopped to chat to her. The friend told Mary that she had heard about of a man called Tom Bates. He was a father of two children, and as his wife had walked out on them all to live with a younger man, he needed someone to live in and look after his children.

Mary got Tom's address and telephone number, and as soon as she got to Gerry's place, she called him. She offered to help look after his children so that he could continue his work, and that she could live in. As Mary had no experience with children, Tom was not too sure to begin with, but agreed to meet and interview her.

As soon as twenty five year old Tom Bates set his eyes on how beautiful Mary was, with or without experience, he wanted her to be his housekeeper. He told her she would be looking after the children, and cooking for them all. At the same time he was thinking, with luck, maybe his bed.

Mary now had a place to stay.

The conditions were that Mary would have free

board but she was to help with the children, cooking, and general house keeping. The fact she could continue her part time job with the hairdressers while the children were at school, suited Mary. She also knew by the way that Tom looked at her, he really fancied her, and she realised that she would possibly soon end up in his bed.

Living like this was much better than it was with those students. On top of that, it was the first time she had a proper home to live in since her father had died.

The family children were Frank age seven, and Denise aged five, because of their fathers cooking, both took to Mary very easily. She was now nineteen, and living with an older man was not a problem for her. The inevitable happened, and she had soon moved into his bed, she even enjoyed his lovemaking. It was not like the sex mad teenagers she had been with in the past.

She lived with the family for about eighteen months and had settled in well; life seemed too good to be true.

One day, before Tom had arrived home from his work, Candy his ex wife, turned up and wanted her husband to take her back. What she did not let on about was the fact that her toy boy had thrown her out for a younger woman.

The children had been delighted to see their mother again and they ignored Mary. Candy took this opportunity to tell Mary the children were getting upset, "So get your things together and get out of my house right away."

Once more Mary McCaferty was homeless. She knew that Gerry had a live in lover, so she went to the local council for help and they directed her to a hostel for unmarried women. Even though she had no children, she was allowed to stay until other accommodation could be found.

The next day Tom Bates contacted Mary and asked her to return home with him, he said that he had told his wife that she should go back to her toy boy that she had been with for the last eighteen months. Tom insisted that their mother was definitely not moving back in with him, even though it had upset the children.

Mary was very happy to agree to go back; however, when she arrived at the house, Frank and Denise did not take to her as well as they had the last time.

They began calling her names and blamed her for their mother going away again. This was making it impossible for Mary to stay and she knew she had to find another home as soon as possible. With them being nasty to her, she could not be happy to live in the home.

Tom was sorry to see her go but he realised that the children had to come first, and he said to her. "I hope that we can remain friends Mary, and perhaps one day we will get back together again." Mary said that she would like to stay friends.

Luckily, she found out that Gerry's girlfriend had

moved on, and Mary was able to go back to sleeping on his couch again.

CHAPTER 6

A gay relationship.

It was about two weeks later that Brenda Gray, a customer in the hairdressers shop, suggested to her that she share her apartment with her. Brenda was ten years older than Mary, who was now coming up for her twenty-first birthday. She did not know that Brenda was gay but when she explained that she would have to share her bed, she realised it.

Mary was thinking that having sex with another female was something she had never contemplated. It had never been on her mind before, but as it meant that she would be sleeping in a bed again, she decided to try it. Maybe she would like it.

The arrangement was going well and Mary had even enjoyed sharing her body with Brenda, she so understood on how to get the best out of a woman's sexual needs. However, for her it just was not the same as sex with a man.

The down side with Brenda was that she was becoming very possessive, she did not like the way that men looked at her partner. However, what was worse for Brenda was when Mary was chatting with other women; she told Mary that she would kill her if she went with another woman. She even banned Mary from celebrating her twenty-first birthday in case one of the partygoers kissed her. However, it did not stop Mary seeing the odd man on the quiet.

For eight months, all went well until one day; someone told Brenda that she had seen Mary with a man. Brenda went crazy; there was no way she was going to put up with that.

As soon as Mary arrived home from her work, Brenda slapped her across the face and told Mary that she would have to give him up or leave.

Mary left.

Mary contacted the local council again, however, this time they could not help her until the following day. Therefore, she asked Gerry if she could spend a few nights on his couch again, and he was pleased to help his little sister.

Mary soon applied to get a full time job in another local hairdresser's shop, who had advertised for a qualified hairdresser and beautician. It would mean much more money, and it was perfect for her.

With Gerry coming up with the deposit for her, she was able to rent a small one bedroom flat. Gerry was also happy to get his flat all to himself again.

Now, without having to depend on lovers for a

roof over her head, she could select her boyfriends. Life at last seemed settled for Mary.

After about six months, Tom Bates came on the scene again, he contacted Mary and told her his wife had come back and taken both the children away. She had found a man who was happy to take on her and her kids, and they were happy to be with their mum again.

Tom was now on his own, and he wanted Mary back, obviously, he was missing sex with a beautiful young woman.

Mary refused to move in and said to him that she was happy in her own little apartment, she told him that he should have tried harder to keep her there and not let the children tell him what to do.

Tom then suggested to her to stay the odd night with him, and if she did that, he would help her with the rent of her own place. Mary McCaferty could not refuse this offer and she lied about the rent she was paying, Tom Bates, unknowingly would be paying almost Mary's full rent.

Spending one night with him, once every couple of weeks or so was agreed, and both were happy.

CHAPTER 7

2002.

Mary's twenty-second birthday.

A twenty-first birthday is always a special one, and Mary, who had not been able to celebrate hers, was intent to make up for it by having her twenty-second birthday, one she would not forget. She contacted the three students that, during the few days she lived with them, had insisted that she have sex with all three of them at the same time.

She called Oliver and told him that she was sorry for leaving them so suddenly after that party, and that as it was her birthday soon, she wanted to make it up to them. She invited them over to her home to celebrate it, and said, "Let's do the party all over again; however this time, as you wanted before, I want all three of you to have me at the same time."

Oliver told her that he would let his friends know and then get back to her.

He contacted his two mates and after he explained

to them what Mary had suggested, Noah and Liam could hardly believe their luck, and readily agreed.

The twenty-second of July could hardly come quick enough for the three men, and they arrived at precisely the time Mary had told them to be there. There was no way they were going to be late for a night of sex with her.

Mary who had been on her phone at the time they had knocked on her door, shouted for them just to enter, they nearly fell over each other trying to get in first. Mary finished her call, by saying to the person on the line, that she had guests. Then she explained to the three men that as she was now into rough sex, she wanted them to slap her around a little bit.

She said, "However, you all have to go naked first, and then we can get started right away."

She continued by saying that they were to take turns to chase her round the room. She explained, "When the chaser catches me I will shout a little and be scratching him a bit as he starts to rip a part of my clothes off. After he manages to get a piece of clothing off, the next one gets to try, and this keeps on going until I am naked, then you can all have me at the same time."

Within seconds, the men were naked and Liam was the first one to begin to run round the room after her. One of the two men sitting on chairs in the middle of the room, laughed as he tripped Mary up, and cheered as she scratched Liam while he pulled at her blouse, and began to rip it off.

After about twenty minutes, and all three had had a go at ripping some of her clothes off, Mary was looking like a rag doll. All she had left on were her bra hanging loose round her neck, and her torn panties. Oliver, Liam and Noah were now looking forward to the sex part of the party.

All of a sudden, Mary's front door burst open and five police officers came rushing in. The three naked men were taken completely by surprise. The evidence was very clear as far as the officers were concerned. When they had entered the room, Mary was laying, almost completely naked on the floor. She was shouting and scratching at Noah, who was leaning over her, slapping her and trying to take off her panties. Her torn clothes were lying all around the room, and Mary appeared to be very distressed. The three men were all arrested and charged with sexual assault.

They started shouting that it was all her idea and that she had invited them to her home to do it. An officer told them that they could tell that to the judge, "You are all nicked." He said.

Mary, who by now was putting on a very good act of being distraught, managed to explain that they were the same men who had forced her into a gang rape once before, and because she had been too frightened to report it at the time, they must have thought that they could do it again.

She said she had heard a knock at the door, and when she opened it, they had all rushed in and attacked her.

One of the officers, a woman, explained that they had had a tip-off, the informant had said that he had seen three men rush into this address, and that there was a female being attacked. Have you any idea who that could be Ms McCaferty?

"I have no idea," she said, "but the neighbours are very nosey, so maybe one of them saw something."

"Lucky for you," said the officer, "do you want to go to the hospital for a check up; you look like you have taken a beating?"

Mary told her that she would call her boyfriend and he would come over right away,

"I will be fine; I will get him to take me there."

The female officer asked her if she was sure, and Mary told her she was fine because they had arrived just in time, and had saved her from being fully sexually assaulted by the men. The WPC offered to stay until her boyfriend arrived, but Mary insisted that she wanted to be left alone as she cleaned up the mess, it was embarrassing enough she said.

With that, the officers left with the three men holding their clothes in front of themselves, and now in handcuffs. They were still shouting and protesting their innocence. One of the police officers escorting them to the police van said, "Aye sure, if you expect me to believe that, I am Santa Claus."

As soon as the police had left her flat, Mary called Tom Bates and told him that their plan had worked well and that his call to the police had been perfectly timed. She also said that she owed him big time, so she would be over to see him within the hour.

Forty minutes later Mary was in Tom's apartment and after welcoming her, he laughed and said that he hoped that he would never get on the wrong side of a certain Ms McCaferty. "Aye," she said, "you do not fuck with a McCaferty and get away with it."

Mary was soon in Tom's bed repaying him for his help in giving those three men what they deserved. After the sex was over and both were dressed, Tom insisted that, as it was her birthday, he was taking Mary out to dinner. She would remember this birthday for a very long time.

In court, all three men were still protesting their innocence, but the Judge told them that the evidence from the five police officers, who attended the scene, far outweighed the explanation from three sex mad young men.

He convicted each of them with one to three and a half years in prison.

CHAPTER 8

Mary McCaferty aged 24.

After a few more years of sharing Toms bed now and again, his son, Frank, wanted to come back and stay with his dad. This was not something that Mary would want to get involved in; she remembered how Frank disliked her and blamed her for the split up of his parents. She told Tom that they would have to arrange to meet at her place from then on; the only reason she said this was the fact that Tom would keep paying her rent.

He happily agreed, and it would mean that ten-year-old Frank would not be aware of his dad and Mary's relationship.

During the four years that he had been seeing Mary, Tom Bates thought that he was the only man to be sharing her bed, but one night when he arrived unexpected, he found out that he was not the only one.

Tom became very jealous, because she was seeing another man at the same time. Moreover, he told her that unless she stopped sleeping with another man, he would no longer be seeing her, and he would not be helping with her rent.

Mary, who by now had been with this business owner for some months, and as he had invited her to stay with him at his apartment, she was moving out anyway. She told Tom to do one; as far as she was concerned Tom Bates was now a memory.

As he left the room, he shouted to her that she was just a devious bastard. Mary shouted back at him, "You may regret you ever said that to me Tom."

CHAPTER 9

James Barr.

James Barr, the businessman, was single and lived in a three-bedroom penthouse apartment that was far superior to the one bedroom flat she had been used to for the last four years. In fact, Mary had never lived in a three bedroom home since the death of her parents.

James, at twenty-eight, was three years older than she was, and he treated her very well. His business was in the clothes retail trade and he was doing well.

Mary had saved a lot of money during the time that Tom Bates had been paying her rent, and now that she was living with another man, she was again living rent-free.

James often bought flowers for Mary, and he was always telling her how much he loved her. How much better could life be, she thought.

That arrangement was fine for about a year and a half, and she had saved up nearly four thousand pounds. She had never had so much money in her life; maybe she could buy herself a car sometime in the future.

All had gone well until James's business began to fail, small clothes shops had begun to find it impossible to compete with the large stores and the internet trade.

James asked Mary to help him financially, but he did not let on just how much he owed. Before she knew it, Mary's bank account began to dwindle, a couple of hundred pounds here and a couple of hundred there, until she had hardly anything left in it. Not only was James in debt at his business, he was well behind with his apartment rent, and he was soon told by the management, to get out of the apartment.

One day while Mary was at work in the hairdressers shop, James, without telling Mary, moved out and disappeared, he had left her having to face the people that he was due money too.

Thankfully, the name on the lease was James Barr, and that the management was trying to find James to get their money. They did not demand the past due payments from Mary, and unless she wanted to rent the place, she just had to collect her belongings and leave immediately. There was no way she could afford this place.

Mary, with no other place to live, and as she had very little of her savings left, was soon back with her brother Gerry, and is again sleeping on his couch.

She is thinking, Even if it is that last thing I do, I am going to get that bastard James.

About three months later, a customer who was getting Mary to cut her hair, told her that she had seen James in Edinburgh. She had been shopping in the Gyle Shopping Centre, a couple of Sundays ago, when she noticed him working in a clothes store there. Mary was delighted to hear this news and she took note of the store.

Mary asked Gerry if he could run her to Edinburgh on the next Sunday, but he had already agreed to take a couple of lads to Dundee for a football match.

As there was a good rail link to Edinburgh, she took a train and then a bus to The Gyle. What she was going to do when she got there she did not know but she just had to make sure it was James.

As she walked round the centre, she passed the store her customer had mentioned, she could see James near the rear of the store serving a customer. She quickly passed on by, and stopped at a coffee shop nearby. Mary decided to wait it out until the shop closed, and then follow him to see where he would go.

She had found out that on Sundays they closed earlier than the rest of the week, so did he have a car or was he using public transport to get to where he was now living?

If it were the first, she would have a problem. However, she knew she had time so she went to another clothes store and bought a headscarf. This would help her to cover her red hair, and then she went back to have a coffee. That would have to last her until the stores closed. Luckily, it was not busy and nobody troubled her to free up the table.

The clothes store closed right on time and within four minutes, James Barr left and headed towards the car park.

"Shit!" Mary says to herself, "I'm going to loose him," however she kept following.

James approached a top of the range, red BMW five series, which Mary recognised as the same car he had had when she stayed with him.

"The bastard," she says quietly to herself, "he still has that car; I bet he owes money on that as well."

As he is getting into the vehicle, she noticed a taxi nearby and runs over to it. She tells the driver to follow the red BMW but do not let the driver know.

"Wow! I have been waiting twelve years for someone to tell me that," the cabby replied.

The route took them into the city district of Morningside and into Autumn Valley Gardens. The taxi moved slowly and stopped fifty meters behind where the BMW had stopped. Mary handed the driver a twenty-pound note and told him to wait. She said that she would need him to get back to the station. The driver said that he was happy to wait, and then watched as Mary got out of his taxi and carefully followed the Beemer driver.

James walked up to a ground floor flat and disappeared inside, Mary took note of the address, then she headed back to her taxi and said to the driver to take her to the station.

On the way there, she began to think of ideas on how to get her own back on James, and what she could do to get her money returned.

Once back at the railway station, she paid the driver for the rest of her fare, and headed to the correct platform for the train back to Kirkcaldy.

By the time Mary arrived back in Gerry's flat, she set about putting her plan into action. The first step was to contact Edin Quality Apartments, who were the agents for the penthouse that she and James had stayed in.

She explained to them that she had found James Barr and that he owed her nearly four thousand pounds. She explained that she had an idea on how to get her money back, and if they helped, they could get their money back as well.

Jim Craig, the manager said, "let me hear your idea Ms McCaferty and we will let you know."

As soon as she finished explaining how to go about it, Jim readily agreed to help Mary.

Friday was always a busy day at The Gyle so this was to be their target day, it would be to their advantage to have many people about. Mary had arranged that morning off her work and three men from the housing agency picked her up for the journey to Edinburgh.

Once in the parking lot, Mary pointed out the BMW to them and then they parked their car about a hundred meters from James's car. The fact that Mary had a spare key for his car was a huge advantage to them. A young man left their car and strode right up to the Beemer; he clicked the key, entered and started the vehicle, then drove out of the parking lot, closely followed by Mary and the other two men.

It had previously been arranged that the Agency would hide the red Beemer in one of the empty lock-ups near to the apartments.

They dropped Mary off at her place and the manager said. "The rest is up to you Mary; we will wait to hear from you, good luck."

CHAPTER 10

The BMW.

Just as James was about to finish his shift in the clothes store, his mobile phone rang, he knew he was not supposed to take personal calls during working hours but as it was near closing time he took the chance.

"Hi James how are you and how is your new job in the clothes store?" There was a short silence before he answered, "Mary what are you calling me for, and how did you know where I am?"

She told him that there was no way she was going to let him get away with taking her savings and not paying them back. James answered by telling her that he had let her stay in his home rent free, so he owed her nothing, in fact she should pay him. Mary replied by reminding him, that he had invited her and that she did not have to pay anything. She continued by telling him that his Beemer had been confiscated and he would not get it back until he paid seven thousand five hundred pounds. James shouted down the phone at her,

"You bitch what the fuck have you done with my

car?"

At that point, Brenda, the store manageress, approached him and told him to hang up and go to her office right away. He had no choice but to do so, but not before Mary overheard the order. She laughed as she closed her own phone.

Meanwhile in the clothes store, James was being told that he should not have been on his phone during working hours and especially should not have been swearing in the store.

He was reprimanded and told if it happened again that he would be sacked. James tried to explain that his ex had just told him that she had stolen his car. His boss cut him off,

"That has nothing to do with this store so keep your personal calls and your bad language out of business hours."

James left the office quietly but raging inside, now he would have to get the public transport home. He knew that he was well behind with the lease payments on the Beemer, and if he contacted the police, they would find that out and definitely confiscate it. Obviously, Mary also knew this fact and that was why she had done this.

As he was sitting on a bus home, his phone rang again, and he could see who that caller was, before she could say anything he said, "You fucking bitch Mary, you nearly got me fired, and where is my fucking car? I called the police and told them you had stolen it so you are in big trouble."

Mary spoke up, "Now now James, remain calm

and I will explain, for a fact I knew you would not call the police as you owe so much on it, so here is what you have to do. Get seven thousand five hundred pounds and send it, or take it, to your old home management people, they will then give you your car back."

"Do not be stupid Mary, I am not due them anything like that, and anyway where would I get that kind of money?"

She replied by telling James that the management, plus what he was due her, came to about seven-thousand pounds and that they were wanting five hundred interest. She said, "if not they are going to turn in your car and claim the reward."
"That car is worth nearly thirty-five grand Mary, you can't seriously let them do that?"

"Yes I can James and they will give me all my money back when they are paid. I did it this way because I knew you would come after me if I did it on my own, this way if anything does happen, those people would contact the police. You have two options James, get the money or lose the car; I will call you in four days." With that said, she ended the call.

James Barr was now getting desperate, where could he get that kind of money without stealing it. He began thinking, maybe by stealing it from the store; I could get my own back on that bitch of a manageress. James was at his wits end and panicking, but how could he steal that much money and get away with it.

First thing on Saturday morning, he arrived early at work so that he could apologise to Brenda Blake, his boss. He told her that he had been so upset by what his ex girlfriend had done; I should not have lost my cool he said. He did know that he had to do quite a bit of crawling if his plan was to work.

He even went as far as saying to her that in a way of apologizing he would take her to lunch and pay for it. Brenda thought for a moment; after all, he had been stressed out by the news from his ex, and he was good looking.

She told him "I have decided to accept your apology and yes you can pay for my lunch."

James gave her his best put on smile and is thinking, well that is step one of my plan going okay.

Just before they went to get something to eat, Brenda excused herself, she took out a small handbag from a larger one she had with her and went to the bathroom; James took this time to have a quick look into the bag she had left. He soon found the store keys and quickly took an impression of the front door one. By the time she returned, James had already put her keys back in her bag.

After they finished lunch, James paid the bill and stood up to hold her chair for her. Brenda thought that was a nice gesture and thanked him, thinking that he is a nice man. They returned to work and James spent the afternoon doing his best to impress.

Closing time came, and as usual, he said goodnight to the others, then with a big smile, he headed to the bus depot for his journey home. Step two done successfully.

Sunday was his day off so he had to wait until the Monday before he could attempt his next move.

Again he was early to work and as Brenda was about to get the days float out for the cash registers, he offered to help her, and in doing so he was able to see the combination to the safe. Step three done.

Because Friday was the stores usual banking day, he knew that he would need to wait a few days before he could be sure there would be plenty in the safe for him.

As there would be approximately sixty thousand in there by Friday, It was his intention to take out ten thousand pounds on the Thursday, and when Brenda took out the cash on Friday for banking, she would not have a clue as to why there was ten thousand short. That would be her problem not his.

In the meantime, he kept up the nice man act.

CHAPTER 11

James panics.

On Tuesday, after he got home from work, Mary called him and asked for the money, she said, "You were told to get it by today James."
He replied by telling her that he was doing his best and hoped to have a loan from a friend on Thursday. "You were told Tuesday James," she shouted at him.

"Christ Mary I'm only asking for an extra two days, surely you could wait that long."

"Well, if not by Thursday, you will not see your car again."

"I will Mary, I promise I will."
Goodbye James, Thursday or else."

James started speaking again then suddenly realised that he was talking to a silent phone. "Fuck you Mary," he shouted out. Even though he knew she could not hear it, he had the satisfaction of saying it.

On Wednesday morning, he again arrived early, just as Brenda was opening the store. Once more, he carefully checked her as she switched off the alarm system, and after hanging her coat up, she opened the safe. Yes, I got the combination right he was saying to himself, I cannot wait until tomorrow.

Thursday was another busy day in the store, which suited James, more money, and the day was passing quickly. Closing time came and he walked out of the store towards the exit of the mall. Hiding behind a pillar, he firstly saw the under manageress leaving and then Brenda came out and locked the door.

James kept well out of the way as she passed and out the exit door. He then walked over to the store, took the copy key out of his pocket, casually but nervously put it in the lock, and turned it. He opened the door and entered the store, closing it behind him. He walked over to the alarm system and switched it off, then adjusted the tape machine for the security camera back five minutes before turning it off. When next turned on, it would record over that bit and would erase the video of him entering the store. The next morning Brenda will think that she had forgotten to switch it on.

He quickly headed to the office and knelt down in front of the safe, using the combination he had written down, it opened easily.

His eyes opened wide as he began to count out ten thousand pounds, fuck it he whispered to himself, another couple of grand would make no difference.

As he was placing the remainder back in the safe, he heard the front door open.

Because she had left her phone on her desk, Brenda was coming back in to get it. James panicked and dropped his bundle of cash on the floor. As he tried to pick it up Brenda walked into the office. "What the hell are you up to James?"

"I, I can explain Brenda."

"You had better have a bloody good excuse because I am going to call the police." She shouted.

Without thinking, James rushed at Brenda and punched her smack in the face. As she fell, the back of her head struck the corner of her desk; she twisted around and landed on the floor with blood pouring from the wound. James now panicked more than ever; he knew that Brenda could identify him so he had to finish her off. He knelt down over her, and put his hand over her mouth trying to suffocate her.

It was then that he heard a voice shouting.

"Hello is there anyone in here?" It was one of the shopping centre security guards, who had spotted the open door. James shouted back,

"In here, someone has broken in and attacked Brenda."

Had he had time to finish Brenda off, he did not know, but if not he was hoping that she would not recover properly from the wound and that she would forget everything.

When he heard the shout, Fred Park the guard, ran into the office, and when he saw James leaning over Brenda, he radioed in to the security office and requested police back up and an ambulance.

He then asked what had happened. James told him that he had come back for his phone that he had left in the store, and found Brenda lying here. Fred told him, "Do not move, there is help on the way."

James was about to get up but Fred told him no, stay there until the police arrive. James realised that he had Brenda's blood all over his hands and that he looked very guilty, so he sprang up and attacked the guard. Fred sidestepped as James, leaped at him; he grabbed James round the neck and the two men struggled and fell to the floor, with Fred's radio falling from his hand. As they were wrestling each other, James grabbed at the radio and smashed it against Fred's face, who immediately recoiled back. James took the opportunity to run and headed for the front door.

That was when he came across Gordon, another security guard. He had heard about the break-in on his radio and came as fast as he could. This time James' luck was out, as he tried to get past Gordon, who was a judo champion; he tackled James, and easily had him on the floor in no time. He got on top of him with his knee in the back of his neck he told him not to move, the cops will be here any minute.

The police and an ambulance arrived within a couple of minutes, James was quickly hand cuffed and then they began inspecting the scene. During this time, the paramedics were doing their best to help Brenda, but she was in a very bad way. They managed to remove a broken tooth from her mouth. Brenda was then rushed to Edinburgh Royal Hospital.

James Barr was arrested and charged with breaking in, assault of two security guards, and Brenda Blake. This would be changed to manslaughter if Brenda died.

During his questioning at the scene, James' phone rang and a sergeant answered it, he could see the name Mary on the screen.

He said, "Hello can I help."
The voice on the other end, asked who it was who had answered her call; Mary knew it was not James.

The Sgt explained that his name was Sergeant Albert Dale from Scottish police, Edinburgh, and that James Barr had just been arrested. He did not go into the details at that point, but asked her to give him her name.

Mary told him her name was Mary McCaferty, and that she was an ex girlfriend of James. "Why has James been arrested?"

Sgt. Dale said that her ex boyfriend had been arrested for assaulting two males and serious assault of a female. James would be taken to Police Scotland headquarters at 49 Drumbryden Drive Edinburgh. He also explained that he would want to question her at a later time. Mary replied that she would be happy to help.

Sgt. Dale thanked her and said, "I will talk to you soon Ms McCaferty, bye."

Now Mary was thinking hard, what do I do now? Wow, if he has been charged with serious assault, he would not get out of prison for a very long time. I have no chance of getting the money now.
Her next move was to call Jim Craig at Edin Quality Apartments, the housing management, and explain to them what had happened. It was agreed by both party's that the Beemer should be returned to the vehicle leasing company and that they would claim the reward for the return of the car. Then Jim told her that when they received the funds, he would send Mary a cheque for four thousand pounds, Mary thanked him and said, "Hope to hear from you soon."

An hour later her phone rang, "Hi Mary here."
"Hello Mary, this is Sergeant Albert Dale from Scottish Police, I am calling to ask you what your relationship is with Mr. James Barr. I know you said he was your ex boyfriend?" She replied by telling him that she had been calling him because he owed her nearly four thousand pounds.
Sgt. Dale laughed a little as he told her that she had little chance of getting it back. "Okay thank you Ms McCaferty that was all I needed to know, I will call again if I need any more info, Bye."

CHAPTER 12

A terrible experience.

Within a few weeks, Mary received a cheque from the housing management who had returned the Beemer to the leasing agency, and they had paid the claim in full. Now she could go out and find another home for herself.

This she did after looking at about five different places. The one she liked best was a one-bedroom ground floor flat in Denton Court. Not only was it near to her brother Gerry in Denton Road, it was fully furnished and in a decent area of Kirkcaldy.

As she had the funds in her bank, she decided to pay six months rent in advance, and as soon as she moved in, she decided to go out and celebrate having her own home again.

That Friday evening saw her in the up market Groves End Bar and Restaurant where she knew many people who went there.

At one point during the night, her eyes met those of a tall handsome man across the other side of the room. He had black hair and a small beard. To Mary he looked about thirty five to forty years old, which meant that he was at least ten to fifteen years more than she was. Age had never bothered her before so why should she let it now, she thought.

She smiled her most sexy smile to him and soon he was over introducing himself as Mike Simpson, a Pharmaceutical representative. The two seemed to be hitting it off well and Mike was insisting on buying the drinks.

The next thing Mary knew was that as she was wakening up, and that she was struggling to try to sit up. She suddenly realised that she was in a bed and that her hands were tied to each side of the bed headboard and her feet to each side of the bottom of the bed, and that she was completely naked.

She took a minute to try to think what had happened and where she was. Her inner thighs were sore and her vagina was aching. What the hell has happened to me? She realised that she had been raped, but who had done it, how and why?

Slowly things started to come back to her; she was remembering the tall dark handsome man, surely it could not have been him, he looked so nice. I would have went to bed with him without this happening, it must have been someone else after she got drunk, but who.

She tried to loosen her hands but they were securely tied with cable ties, God I hope I have not been left here to die. What she did not know was that the culprit was in fact the tall man and he had a sadistic mind. He got his satisfaction by playing with himself as he was playing rough with a woman's private parts.

Mary heard a door open and a hooded figure came into the room. She shouted. "Who are you, and what do you want with me," The man spoke quietly and told her to shut up or he would kill her. You are my slave he told her, and you will do as you are told if you want to live. I am going to put a blindfold on you now so please do not try to resist, then I will have a little fun with you again. Mary started to plead with him so he slapped her on the face and said shut up bitch or I will gag you as well. After the blindfold was on she felt his hands on her lower body, he was pushing something into her vagina and it was hurting her so much that she called out. The man immediately put a gag on her and told her that she had been warned.

Whatever it was that was inside her was now being moved around and hurting her. Moreover, as it was being used, she could hear him making noises. It was apparent to Mary that this man was playing with himself and eventually by the noise he gave out he had satisfied himself. She could feel something warm on her breasts and realised what it was, but she was helpless to do or say anything.

Soon she could hear water running and then a warm cloth or sponge washing her body; obviously, the person was getting rid of any evidence.

The voice told her that he was about to remove her gag so that she could get a drink, so do not shout out or say anything. Mary nodded to comply, at the same time thinking that the assailant had a strange accent, it was the way he had pronounce the word 'about', and it sounded like 'aboot,' to her. With the blindfold still on, he held a glass to her mouth, as her throat was very dry, she was happy to drink the water.

What she did not know was that there was more of the drug in the water.

When Mary wakened up, she was half sitting, half lying on a park bench, and trying to think how she got there. After about thirty minutes or so, she started to wonder if she had got drunk at the pub, and had slept in the park all night.

She quickly felt herself ache between her legs and then remembered lying naked and tied to a bed. Now Mary was not even sure what day it was, never mind where she was. A female jogger approached the area near to where she was, so Mary shouted and asked her for help.

After Mary gave her a very brief summary of her experience, the Jogger called the police and an ambulance. She stayed with Mary until help arrived, then wished her all the best and continued her run. After the ambulance arrived and the paramedics had a chat to Mary, they suggested taking her to the hospital.

WPC Andrews, who had also attended, accompanied Mary to the hospital, where she was thoroughly checked out and given some medication. A doctor explained that she had been what they called date raped, and there was no way that she could possibly have remembered what was happening to her while she was under the influence of it.

As it was now Sunday, Mary had lost a day and a half, but what she did remember about the interval in between, was that she must have obviously been doped a second time. He had done that so she could be released without knowing who the attacker was.

The female police officer, who had gone to the hospital with her, took notes from the doctor and then from Mary. She told the WPC that the man she remembered being in the Groves End Bar with, had black hair and a small beard, in addition, the assailant had a strange accent, it was specifically noted that he had pronounced the word about, more like aboot, which was one word that Mary had remembered.

The WPC asked her if she wanted to make a statement, but Mary told her that all she wanted at that moment was to go home.

WPC Ann Andrews offered to take Mary home and the offer was gratefully accepted. When they reached Mary's home in Denton Court, Ann asked her again about a statement but she refused. She said that she was still trying to remember everything that had happened, so she would report it the following day.

That evening she telephoned her boss at the hairdressers, and explained what had happened to her.

Her boss straight away told Mary to take at least two days off then let her know how she felt. Mary thanked her and said that she was hoping to get back soon. However, she did need an extra day to recover, before she felt like standing behind a customer's seat in the shop, and her boss was fine with that. She knew how good Mary was at her job.

Come Monday morning she had decided not to go to the police, they already knew there had been a rape. As she could not offer any further information about the man, she thought that was enough and she wanted to try to forget it.

When she got back to her work, it was difficult to keep her mind on her work, so she really had to concentrate hard on what she was doing.

It was constantly on her mind as to how she could have let that happen to her, if I meet that bastard again he would get what is coming to him.

A couple of weeks later, as she was sitting reading a book, the television was on in the background. Mary had always thought that it was comforting to have the TV on and turned down a little. Suddenly one of the persons talking sounded very familiar to her and she thought she had heard that "about" word. Quickly she turned the sound up and listened carefully. Five minutes passed before she heard it again, and it definitely sounded like aboot.

She looked at the TV and saw this grey haired clean-shaven man, no she thought, that is not him. The man who she had met in the bar had black hair and a beard. However the more he talked the more she thought that it was him. She got her mobile phone out and as soon as there was a close up of the doctor on the screen, she took a picture then continued watching the rest of the program. When it finished, the interviewer thanked Dr. Martin Symons, and when the credits came up on the TV screen, it read,

Thanks to Dr. Martin Symons
from the University of Toronto, Canada.

Mary jumped up in the air shouting at no one other than herself, "I'm sure that's him, that's the bastard who got me; it was a Canadian accent that I had recognised."

Straight away Mary printed out an eight by four black and white paper copy of the picture, then she took a pencil and darkened the hair, and she added a beard. Bloody hell, it is a spitting image of him; I've got him, now what? She was saying to herself.

She started by putting his name into Google, and up came a picture of Dr. Symons. He had qualified as a gynecologist at the University of Toronto Canada, and eventually became a top advisory at various other Universities' throughout Canada, before continuing his profession in the UK. Dr Symons had based himself and his family in Edinburgh, Scotland.

He was now living with his wife and two children in Morningside Park Lane in the city. Bastard, he is a right fucking weirdo, if I went to the police, they would never believe me. With my word against his, they would say I was insane. I do not know how, but one way or another I am going to ruin his career and his marriage.

Mary thought about it for nearly an hour before coming up with a plan. That plan was very much relying on a lot of luck but she had to try, after all she had promised herself.

She was guessing that he would be so confident in himself that he would do it again, but in another town. She looked out a map and took note of all the larger towns around Edinburgh, Christ I did not realise there were so many she thought. However, she wrote them all down and then had to decide where to start. It was going to be like looking for a needle in a haystack, but it had to be done, even although it took her years. She suggested to her brother that he go with her and that she would pay his way, Gerry was always keen to help his sister so he agreed.

Throughout the next three and a half months, He and Mary spent their Friday nights in high-class bars in the towns on her list. Gerry was beginning to get a little despondent and he started to wonder if they would every find him. Therefore, Mary went back to studying Dr Symons' schedule. On taking notes, she noticed that he had weekends away on the first weekend of the month, wow this could be the break that she needed. This would be his excuse for having time away from his wife, and give him the opportunity to snare a victim.

Mary now knew that she, along with Gerry, had to continue their search, as it would only be once a month. Gerry agreed to the new schedule.

Two months later, they were in Dalkeith on the East side of Edinburgh. On this particular Friday night, in the place that she had selected, there was a convention for a young women's business group in a local hotel, somehow Mary felt lucky.

It was near to nine thirty when a large group of women came into the bar, and surprise surprise, a tall black haired man with a beard followed them in. Mary had put on a blonde wig to conceal her red hair, that along with keeping Gerry between the man and herself, she could remain unnoticed, and she knew he would be watching the group of women. Very soon, they noticed the man approach a beautiful woman who had obviously been looking at him. That was his key to move in.

Mary kept her eye on the pair and when she had finished her drink, the man ordered her another one. At that point, the man knew that he could not slip the drug into her drink without her noticing, he would have to wait his chance, and that came just as she had finished her Gin and tonic. The woman spoke to the man and then headed to the ladies powder room, with Mary close behind her. The man walked up to the bar to order another drink it was his ideal opportunity to spike her drink.

CHAPTER 13

The Trap.

Mary gave the woman time to do what she came in to do, and then spoke to her, she explained as quickly as she could about the man she was sitting with.

The woman, whose name was Janice Dean, at first did not believe what Mary was saying, she thought that she was a jealous ex of his.

Mary then, from her handbag, produced a couple of pictures of the man, one as he was as the Doctor, and the other after Mary had done her artwork.

When Janice saw the differences and how alike they were, it was enough, what do you think I should do, she asked. Mary told her that if her brother gave them the thumbs up as the left the Ladies, they would know that the man had doped her drink.

After Janice sat down, Mary would get Gerry to create a diversion, and when the man looked round to see what had happened, you are to swap the drinks around. After about five or ten minutes you should see his eyes going a little bit glazed, that is when you touch your right ear. We will then come over and join you. The rest I will explain then.

Janice returned to her table and apologized to the man for taking so long at the ladies, but it had been busy she told him.

The man who had called himself Mike, told her no problem, please sit down and enjoy your drink. Janice lifted the glass and said cheers as they chinked their glasses together; she put it to her mouth and pretended to take a sip.

The next thing they knew was that a man had walked past their table, as he did he stumbled and knocked into a table next to them. It had turned over creating a big disturbance. Mike turned round to see what had happened and Janice quickly swapped the glasses over.

Over the next few minutes, Janice sipped at her drink and Mike was getting a little frustrated, she should have been nearly finished her drink by now, not just sipping it, and he should have her in his control by now.

He told her to drink up and he would order another one, Janice thought that he was starting to look a little strange so she lifted her glass and said,

"Bottoms up,"

Mike smiled and did the same and ordered another Gin and Tonic. Within a few minutes, Janice put her hand up to her ear, which was the signal.

Mary and Gerry walked over and said to Mike,

"Hi I hope you don't mind if we join you,"

Mike smiled as he said, "Please do." Obviously, with the hypnotic state he was in, he did not recognise Mary.

From this moment on Mike, aka Martin, would have no clue as to what he was doing for the next few hours. Janice whispered to Mary and thanked her for saving her, but she was told by Mary, "you are not done yet lass; I presume you would like to get involved in a little pay back time."

"Definitely," Janice replied.

As the two men chatted, Mary quietly explained what she had in mind and Janice agreed. She suggested that they use her place as it was the nearest, and then said to Mike that they should all go to her place and have a bit of fun. This brought a big yes from him, and the drug had obviously made him forget his original plan. They finished their drinks and left the bar. Janice directed Gerry to her home. Once there, they talked Mike into stripping naked and to lie on the bed. When he did this, Gerry helped them to tie his hands and arms to the framework, and the women set about shaving his complete body.

Gerry saw that the women wanted to take full control so he stood back and let them get on with it. While Mary finished shaving his head, Janice went and fetched a black permanent ink felt pen into the bedroom. Under instructions from Mary, she took hold of his private parts and began colouring them with the ink, if Dr. Martin wanted black hair, he was getting black, maybe not where he intended though. She then handed the pen to Mary who had finished shaving his head; she wrote the word prick, on top of it, and slightly to the back, where, if he looked in a mirror he would not see it. Next, she wrote in bold letters on his tummy, Mary and Janice was here, kiss kiss kiss in the form of three letters, X X X, and then they both signed it.

All this time Dr. Martin Symons, just lay there and said nothing, as far as he was concerned he was having fun with two women. He was un-aware as to what they were up too. As soon as they were finished, they got him dressed and back into Gerry's van. They drove back to the pub area and scouted around until Mary spotted what she thought was his Beemer, She clicked his car keys and the lights flicked on and off so she knew it was definitely his. After settling the doctor into the drivers' seat, Gerry put the key in the ignition, and they drove away.

Janice suggested that all three spend the night at het flat as she had two bedrooms and it was near-est. In fact, if they did that they could celebrate with a few drinks. Gerry quickly said that it was a good idea, as he had not had an alcoholic drink all night. Janice's place it was then, and a little while after they arrived, Mary made a telephone call.

At three o'clock that morning, a police officer tapped on the car window and wakened Martin. He was still in a bit daze but he did open his door.

"Well, well, well, what do we have here Doctor Martin Symons; I think you have been a naughty boy, haven't you?"

Martin asked, "How do you know my name."

The officer replied by telling him that they had had a tip off about a drunk driver, and that they had already done a check on the vehicle before wakening him up. The officer asked the doc to climb out of his car, and as he did, he noticed the writing on top of his head.

He continued by saying, "by the looks of you sir, I think that you have had far too much to drink, it must have been quite a party sir. Did you know that someone had written something on the top of your head?"

"What, how could they have, I have a full head of hair."

"I am sorry sir but you are completely bald and you have the word prick written up there."

The officer could hardly keep from laughing when he said that.

Dr. Martin looked in his rear view mirror but could not see anything, and he still could not explain what he had been doing. Doctor Martin Symons was arrested and charged with being drunk in charge of a vehicle.

His car was secured and he was placed in the rear of the police car, and then taken to Newbattle Road, Police station, Dalkeith, where he would spend the rest of the night.

In his cell he slowly began to question himself as to what had happened to him, but how could it, he was asking himself. Especially having his head shaved. He had no idea what else had been done to his body, but would soon find out more when he went too relieve his bladder.

At six thirty in the morning, a police officer called Dr. Symons' home and spoke to his wife. He explained to her that he was calling from the police station in Dalkeith. After relaying to her that her husband had been arrested for being drunk in charge of a vehicle, Mrs. Symons said, "It cannot be my husband he is at a convention in Coventry." They informed her that it definitely was her husband and by the looks of him, he had been at a wild party. "What do you mean, at a wild party, He told me that he was going to Coventry, and you say he is in Dalkeith?"

"Yes Mrs. Symons, he is in one of our cells at the moment, and someone needs to come and pick him up. His car was secured by an officer at the scene, so it can be recovered in Forth Street, Dalkeith."

Mrs. Symons told the officer that she would be there in about two hours, and that her husband would have to wait in his cell for a while longer. She said, "Maybe he will want to stay there longer by the time I have finished with him."

The officer was smiling as he told her that he would see her soon.

9 am. Dalkeith.

Mrs. Gayle Symons arrives by taxi in Forth Street, Dalkeith, to collect the family vehicle. Good job I had a spare set she thought. She paid her taxi then set the sat nav in the Beemer to find the police station. Once there, her husband was brought into the waiting room, she took one look at him and shouted at him, "you have a lot of explaining to do Martin, Get in the car now." Obviously so far, Martin had not had to relieve himself.

CHAPTER 14

Morningside Edinburgh.

On the way home to Fifty One, Morningside Park Lane, very little was said by either of them, although there was certainly a lot of thinking going on.

The journey took twenty minutes, but it seemed much longer to Martin, he was not looking forward to getting home. As soon as they entered their two-story town house, Gayle set about him,

"What the fuck have you been up to Martin?"

All he said was that he could not remember anything, "I must have been drugged."

"Drugged! Fucking drugged, you were supposed to be in Coventry, I will give you fucking Coventry. Why were you in Dalkeith, and who drew prick on your head?"

This was when Martin remembered that the police had told him of the writing on his head,

"I better go for a shower and wash it off," he said.

Still swearing and asking questions, Gayle followed him up to their bedroom. She was suddenly speechless as Martin removed his clothes.

"Oh fuck" came from Martins mouth, "I do not know how that happened, honest dear I have no idea."

What confronted Gayle was Martin standing there almost naked, not only was his privates blackened, but also written on his body were two names, Mary and Janice was here, X X X, and the signatures of the two women.

"Jesus Christ Martin, you are well and truly fucked now, who the hell are Mary and Janice, and what have you been up to with them?" Martin just stood there thinking, he had absolutely no explanation, other than that he had been having a drink with a female called Janice, in a bar last night, and who was Mary? "I have no idea; I promise," He shouted. However, Gayle had other ideas,

"You bastard Martin, you were supposed to be in Coventry, but instead you have been with a couple of fucking tramp bitches and they got you drunk, well you can pack your case now and get out."

He began pleading his case and telling her that he needed her help as he had a television interview on the Thursday.

"You are getting no help from me you cheating bastard, go get your bitches to help you."

She gave him one almighty slap that nearly knocked him off his feet. "You better be out of here before lunch time. Start packing now and take your prick head and black dick with you."

Martin went into the shower and soon found out that the ink would not wash out, Christ what am I going to do, a shaved head, no home and an interview on TV to come in four days time. He washed as best he could, got dressed, and found a cloth cap in a drawer. With that on his head and two suitcases full of his clothes, before he headed out the door, he tried one more time to plead with his wife he had no luck, all he heard was, fuck off.

With the Best Western Hotel being closest to his home, he decided to stay there hoping that his wife would ask him back.

Thursday 6.30 pm.

Mary and Janice had decided to keep in touch with each other and when Janice got a call from her, she was very happy. "Hi Janice, you are never going to believe this but that creep Martin is going to be back on TV tonight at half past seven. I just heard an announcer say earlier that Dr. Martin Symons had decided to go ahead with his pre-arranged interview, even though he had had some upsetting personal things going on at home. It appeared that he had separated from his wife and children only a few days previously, but he was being very brave to continue with the show."
Janice was surprised, but said I must watch it."
Mary said, "Me too, talk later."

Independent Television, 7.30pm.
The Jamie Goodyear show.

The show begins with Jamie announcing to his

live audience, "Good evening ladies and gentlemen, we are so lucky to welcome back a distinguished speaker with us tonight, please welcome Dr. Martin Symons."

As the crowd was clapping to welcome the doctor, Mary watched as a grey haired Dr. Symons walked onto the platform. He was welcomed by Jamie who went on to announce that Dr. Symons was an expert on Gynecology, and later in the program, he would be taking questions from the audience and by telephone. Wow, thinks Mary, I can hardly wait for that, he is going to get a call from me.

During the early part of the program, Dr Symons was questioned on his career, and why he entered Gynecology. His answer was that in his early career he had always found that women were often afraid to go to see a doctor when there was something wrong with their bodies. He continued, but they really should not be afraid, they should never have to be embarrassed to have their vaginas examined by a doctor, especially a male doctor. He went on to say, we are as capable of checking the female body as much as a female doctor.

Mary shouted at her TV screen, "Aye but that does not give you the right to fucking abuse them you bastard.

The interviewer then asked for questions from the audience and that they would take phone calls in a few minutes.

Mary was on to it in a flash, after it had rang for

a few minutes her call was answered. A receptionist asked her name and what her question to Dr. Symons would be; this was so that they would not be expecting any crank calls.

Mary told the receptionist what her first name was, and she wanted to know what the doctor would advise a woman to do if she had been sexually assaulted. Should she go see a doctor about it as soon as possible, and if she did, if the doctor was a man, could she insist on a female doctor? The receptionist said to her that she had posed a good question, and she would be fourth in line to talk to the doctor. It could take a few minutes because of the others in front of you, and it would depend on how long the doctor took to chat with them. She informed Mary, however I will pre warn you when you are about to go on.

"Thank you." said Mary.

Twenty Three, Morningside Park Lane, Edinburgh.

During the program, Ashley Blair was watching the television with her husband, Chief Inspector Charles Blair. They were near neighbours of the Symons's who lived at number Fifty-One. She was saying that there was something strange about that doctor.

"What is that?" her husband asked.

She told him that she had seen the program a few months ago, and they announced then that the doctor would be on the program again in a few months time. Back then, his hairstyle looked nothing like it was now.

"Don't be silly dear; he must have just had it styled lately for the TV."

She said to him, "I had seen him just a week and a half ago as he was walking to his car, and he had a good head of hair then and it was exactly the same as it was when he was on TV last time. It looks like a wig he has on now; remember dear I used to be a hairdresser before I married you, so I should know."

It took about twenty minutes before it was Mary's turn, and the cue came, you are on now Mary. Jamie Goodyear came on first, "Good evening Mary; I hear that you have a very interesting question for Dr. Symons, go ahead."

Mary said, "Good evening Dr. Symons," and then she repeated the same question she had said to the receptionist. Dr. Symons took a second or two, and then answered, "This is a very interesting question that you have asked Mary, do I presume that you have, in the past, been sexually assaulted yourself?"

Mary could hold on no longer, she spoke out,

"Fine you know it was you Dr. Symons, you fucking pervert that was why, after shaving your head, I wrote prick on top it, and we coloured your dick bl..."

The director cut off the phone call.

Jamie Goodyear was taken aback by the question and he started to apologise to the doctor for the abusive call. All the same, he could not help but look at the doctors' head, and saw what looked like a poor looking wig on it. Jamie was thinking, could the caller be right.

Doctor Symons announced that as he was in shock at such a terrible accusation, it might be best to end the interview right away.

The program director had already cut to the adverts, and as he did, Dr. Martin Symons rose from his seat. As he stormed off the platform a female stagehand, Denise Ryder, who had thought that there was something strange about the way the doc looked, from how he had done previously. She 'accidently' bumped into him and knocked his wig off, as he bent down to pick it up, she could see the faint word in black bold letters, PRICK, on top of his head.

Doctor Martin Symons shouted that he was going to sue the program, and was putting his wig back on as he ran out of the studio as fast as he could.

At the same time as he was doing that, Gerry was on the phone to Mary.

"Well you certainly put the cat among the pigeons there sis that was hilarious."

Mary told him that the Doc had deserved it, "I hope that he gets struck off now."

"Quite right," replied Gerry, "at least his marriage is done for, so is his career now we hope."

Mary said that her phone was buzzing, "It must be Janice on the line, I will call you back." Gerry said "Bye talk soon sis." and he ended the call.

Right away Mary had Janice on the line, who sounded like she was crying with laughter. Eventually she managed to tell Mary how much she had enjoyed what had gone on during the program. Both women talked on the line for the next fifteen minutes before ending their call.

Back in Twenty Three, Morningside Park Lane, Ashley and Charlie Blair were sitting in front of their TV, just looking at each other. "What was that all about then?" asked Charlie.
"Told you before that he was a strange man dear, I wonder if the woman who called in was right. You should check up on that when you get back to work tomorrow dear."
Charlie thought for a moment then told his wife that he would, after all she was good at judging people.

Friday am. Scottish Police,
49 Drumbryden Drive, Edinburgh.

Chief Inspector Blair set about making enquiries as to what had happened on the TV program last night. He knew it had taken place at the Independent Television, Studios, Edinburgh, so it should be no problem contacting them.
He spoke to Sergeant Bert Dale and told him to contact the TV station and see what information they could come up with.
By lunchtime, Sgt Dale had the information his boss wanted, and conveyed it to him. It contained

the all the details of a Doctor Martin Symons, including his University history, and what had occurred during the TV program. A copy of the tape of the telephone call from a female called Mary, and the details ended with a statement from Denise Rider, a stagehand who had suspected something strange about the Doctor and about his hair.

After the two had sat listening to the short tape, CI Blair said that they should try to find out who this Mary is, and if this man has assaulted her in the past, then we need to know how she had not reported it. I think Bert, that, I will contact the University of Toronto and see if they had any information on this Doctor.

"I want you to go and interview this Denise Rider Bert, ask her if she had meant to bump into the doctor. She had said that she had accidentally done it, but I do not believe that. Also, ask her if she was positive about what she saw on top of the Docs head. If so, we will have to bring her in to get a proper statement from her."

"Will do sir," replied Bert.

The CI continued, "As Canada is five hours behind us, I will have to wait until this afternoon to call there. Therefore, in the meantime I will contact the Edinburgh Evening Telegraph and get them to put an appeal in this evening's paper for the woman called Mary, and ask her to contact us at Police Scotland. I hope that she will see it and come forward."

Bert said, "Aye Sir and what about the Doctors

wife, she must know something. I think that was maybe what the private family problem could have been."

"You are correct Bert, I will see if I can talk to her today."

CHAPTER 15

News from Canada.

CI Blair spoke to the editor of the 'Tele,' as the Evening Telegraph newspaper was known locally. He said he was happy to oblige as it could mean a good story for his paper. He also suggested that if this Mary did not want to talk to the police directly, she could call him at the newspaper. CI Blair agreed that it was a good idea. "Thank you," he told the editor.

The phone rang at Fifty-One Morningside Park Lane. "Hello the Symons residence."
"Good morning Mrs. Symons my name is Chief Inspector Charles Blair from Scottish police, you may know me, as my wife and I live just up the street from you. I would like to speak to you about your husband and I could do that here or at your home whichever is best for you." Gayle was a bit taken aback, but she replied, "Oh hello Chief Inspector, yes I know who you are, how can I help you, my husband and I are not together anymore."
"Please call me Charlie Mrs. Symons, that way it sounds friendlier, as the police need to talk to you

and ask a few questions, I thought that maybe it would be easier for you talking to someone you know."

"I am not to sure about the police coming to my home Charles, and please call me Gayle. I think that I would be a bit nervous about going to the police station as well, so is it possible for me to meet you at your home?"

"Absolutely Gayle, if you want to go there in about fifteen minutes I will call my wife to expect you and I will get there in about forty minutes, so that will let you have time to relax with my wife first." Gayle agreed and told the CI that she will go round there soon. They ended the call.

Charlie then phoned his wife and said to her to expect a visitor, and he explained why.

"See you soon dear," he said as they ended their call.

CI Blair called into the office on his way out and spoke to Brenda, the secretary. "Hi Brenda, I want you to try to find a telephone number and a contact name for the police in Toronto, Canada. Also the same for the University of Toronto, it's at 27 Kings College Circle." He knew that after reading about Martin Symons in the report he received from the TV director. He told her that he would be back in a couple of hours, and he expected the information on his desk when he got there. Brenda said that she would do her best. If you need help lass, get the help of a PC, I am sure there is one or two around that need some office experience.

Fifteen minutes later Gayle arrived and Ashley warmly welcomed her, she introduced herself, and then told her to sit on the settee and make herself at home, "I will make us a cup of tea while we wait on Charles."

The two women were getting on well and Gayle's only mention of her husband was to say that they had parted. When Charles arrived home, he said hello to Gaye, sat in his chair and began chatting to her. Ashley said, as it was none of her business, she would leave the two to talk. However, Gayle asked her to stay, as it gave her some comfort with another female there.

Charles began by telling her that this meeting was off the record, so he would not be reporting anything she says. He went on, the police were now sure that her husband may be in serious trouble and that they would appreciate any help that she could give them.

Charles did say that if he thought that some of the information was required, she might have to accept officers going to her home, or she to go to the station to make a statement. "As I promised you, today's meeting is for information only," he said.

Gayle thanked him then said to them that because of a previous accusation against Martin, which was the reason for them coming to Scotland. She continued, "A woman in Toronto had said that Martin had sexually assaulted her under the influence of drugs, she had said that she had only been partly under the influence but still, she was not able to resist him, however she did manage to recognise him. Of course, Martin denied it all, and after a month or so, the female retracted the charge and stated that she may have been wrong. Martin was then cleared."

Gayle said that she had told her husband that they could not stay there as long as the neighbours were wagging their tongues at us. She continued, "Because my grandparents were originally from Scotland and our daughter, Claire, is at St. Andrews University, that is why we came here. While we were getting all our personal things sorted out for the move, Martin told me that we had lost a fortune on the stock market. At the time, I did not connect it with what he had been accused off with by the woman, but now I believe that he must have paid her off, and not lost our savings.

When he was arrested drunk in charge of his car in Dalkeith, I had to go and get him from the police station, that was when I saw his head had been shaved, and the word Prick had been written in indelible ink on top of it."

Her face reddened when she said that.

"I was furious enough at that, but it got a lot

"What happened there?" asked Charles.

Gayle went on; "When Martin stripped off to have a shower and to wash his head, I got the biggest shock of my life, I could hardly believe what was written on his body. In bold letters were the names, Mary and Janice, X X X and they had signed their names underneath. They had also used the black ink pen on his testicles and his penis they were completely blackened. I shouted at him to get out." Gayle broke down at that point.

Ashley rose from her chair and sat next to Gayle on the settee; she put her arm around her and comforted her.

Charlie sat quiet for a minute to give her time to compose herself, and then he said, "Gayle, what you are telling me is very serious. I know you do not want officers at your home, and you are not happy to go to the station. What I would suggest is that I get two police officers to come here to our home and get a proper statement from you. We need to catch your husband before he does it again to another woman, and I don't think that you would like that to happen, would you?"

Gayle sobbed, "No I would not be able to live with myself if I let that happen Charles. Yes I will do a statement for you, as long as Ashley stays with me during it." Ashley told her that she would be happy to help.

Charles called the station and a WPC, along with a CID officer were assigned to come and take the statement. He then excused himself, as he had to get back to the station to telephone Canada.

As he entered the station, Brenda shouted, "It's all on your desk sir." He replied, "Thank you Brenda, I knew you could do it."

Once in his office he called Sergeant Dale and

asked him to come and inform him as to the girl Denise Rider at the TV station. When the Sergeant arrived, he told his CI that Denise had stated that she had suspected that there was something very strange about the Doctor, it had been the way he looked at her that made her feel funny. He had even made a suggestion about a date with her. Denise had said that the creep was old enough to be her granddad. She had thought that he was wearing a wig and knew that it was not there on his first appearance on the show. When she had heard Mary mention that she had shaved the doctors' head that was when she decided to see for herself. Sergeant Dale said that she told him that she did bump into him on purpose to knock the wig off, and when the doctor bent down to pick it up, she saw the word prick right on top of his head.

I talked to the TV program people sir, and told them what Denise had done was very wrong, but at least it had proved that the caller, Mary, had something that she needed the public to know. I asked them not to reprimand Denise for her actions and they agreed.

"Thanks Bert that is great news," and he went on to tell him what the doctors wife had told him, then said, "What we need to do now is to find Doctor Martin Symons and bring him in, see if you can find out his whereabouts Bert. While you are doing that, I am going to phone University of Toronto, and the police there, so make sure I am not disturbed Bert."

"Aye sir "came the reply.

Just over an hour later, CI Blair had been able to talk with both the University and the Toronto Police.

The Dean at the University had informed him that he remembered the situation and they had suspended him at the time. However, after Doctor Symons was cleared, they had reinstated him, but he had been requested to resign. If he did so, they would take no action on his record. The Dean did think that there might have been something in the accusation but as he was cleared, they had to believe him. CI Blair wrote in his notes that the Dean had been thanked for his assistance.

Next was the report from Toronto Police, Detective Inspector Drew Monroe was the contact, as he had had a major role in the investigation on Doctor Symons. He remembered the case well, and was sure that the woman had been paid off, but they could not prove it. It had been noted that Dr, Symons had made a huge loss on the stock market but there was nothing to connect that, and the victim retracting her statement charging the Doc.

He said that the amount involved was in the region of two hundred and fifty thousand Dollars. It was no wonder that the woman took his money, if only we could prove it. DI Drew Munroe asked Charles, if and when the Doctor was finally caught, could he get in touch and let him know. He had said that he would love it, and that it would let him put a proper end to his case as far as he was concerned.

Charlie agreed that he would, but that they needed to find the Doc first. Drew ended with, "Good luck Charlie."

CI Blair asked Sgt. Bert to come back in, and when he did, Charles asked how he was getting on with locating the Doctor. Bert told him that he had not found out where the Doc was. So far, they have been contacting family friends and acquaintances.

Well we will just keep searching my friend, and hope the newspaper report comes up with something tonight."

"Yes sir."

CHAPTER 16

Seven fifteen, pm. the Evening Telegraph had been delivered to Twenty Three, Morningside Park Lane, Edinburgh.

Charlie and Ashley Blair had just finished their dinner, and he went to his front door to pick up the paper. After he returned to his chair, he read it, and soon saw the report. He mentioned it to his wife, and told her what it said; she then called Gayle to let her know.

"Please read it out to me Ashley, I do not get the paper."

The two-column report read:-

After a disturbance during a talk show program on TV last night, Edinburgh Police are looking for a woman to come forward. Her name is Mary and she is known to be involved in the police enquiries. They are also looking for a Doctor Martin Symons to come forward, as he was the recipient of the abuse on the program.
The police are regarding this as a serious case and they

would love to hear from these people or someone who may know them.

The editor of this newspaper has kindly offered to help the police, by saying that if the informant is frightened to call the police they can contact him at the newspaper. All conversations will be treated with utmost discretion.

Gayle said, "Well we can't do much more, we need to rely on the women to get in touch. Thanks for letting me know."

Ashley told her that Charles had said that even if they find your husband they could not arrest him until they had witnesses; the police need those women to come forward.

Gayle replied. "I hope so Ashley,"

"We all do, I will let you know if we hear more, talk soon, bye."

Seven thirty, Dalkeith.

Janice Dean had just got home and set about getting her dinner ready. While she waited on it cooking, she picked up the Evening Telegraph to have a quick look through it. Suddenly a news column caught her eye, bloody hell, I had better call Mary, she said to herself.

Mary was busy with a customer at the time her phone rang, so she let it go to voice mail. Janice gave her a brief rundown on the report and asked Mary to contact her soon.

About half an hour later, she got that call. "Hi Jan-

ice, as soon as I listened to your message I got our junior hairdresser to run out and get the paper, we need to think about this. I am heading home soon so I will contact you when I get there, that will give me time to think. Let me know what you think, and we will decide together, it has to be a decision that we are both happy with."
"Okay Mary, I will let you call me later, Bye."

Seven forty-five, Friday evening, a certain Doctor, in the Best Western hotel, Edinburgh, was reading the paper. Shit, I am going to have to get out of here as soon as possible, good job I did not use my real name when I booked in.

Doctor Martin Symons packed his two cases and caught the Edinburgh express bus to Glasgow. He planned to head south from there and merge into the crowds of a busy city, and while he sat on the bus, he was trying to decide which one.

He was even thinking that he would be able to pick up a few nice young women in a big city. As soon as he arrived in Glasgow, he headed for the train station. Bought a ticket and as he had two hours to wait on his train, he went for a coffee. With the ticket in his pocket, he would be able to get off the train at any place that he wanted to.

As he was traveling south, he would decide which city, and with another new name, Malcolm Sharp, Martin Symons could just disappear. By using that name, the initials on his brief case would match in.

Meanwhile in Kirkcaldy, one of his previous victims was talking on the telephone to her friend. "Well Janice, what do you think we should do?"
She replied, "It is really up to you Mary; after all it was you who saved me from getting raped by him. Whatever you decide I will back you all the way, but I would like to see him in jail so that other women are safe."

Mary agreed, "I will call in tonight, do you think the police or the newspaper?" Janice thought for a moment then told her that she felt that the police would be best; the paper may want to get a story from the two of them before they contacted the cops. Mary said that she would call the police right away.

Eight-thirty pm. St. Brycedale Road, Kirkcaldy, a Constable in the police station takes the call. After Mary told him why she was calling, the Constable connected her to the duty sergeant, Lee Davis. He said that he was very pleased to hear from her, and could he take her number. Lee told her that he was under instructions to let the Chief Inspector at Scottish Police, Edinburgh know immediately he heard from anyone regarding the case.

Sgt Lee said that a CI Blair would call her after he had called Edinburgh and told him you were in touch. Mary said okay I will like that, she then told Sgt. Lee her number then said bye.

Ashley took the call at the Blair household and as

soon as she heard what Sgt. Lee had to say, she shouted on her husband.

CI Blair took note of the number and thanked his Sergeant.

Mary was sitting waiting on the call, but she still jumped when her phone rang.

"Hello Mary, this is Chief Inspector Charles Blair from Edinburgh Police."

He knew that he needed to keep the call as friendly as possible. He continued, "I would like to thank you for calling us, and can you please let me know your second name."

She told him, "at the moment just call me Mary." she wanted to chat first before she found out what she had to do.

"Okay Mary, just as you wish, obviously I would have preferred to talk personally with you, but we will take it step by step. I know this must be very difficult for you." Mary told him that she was in Kirkcaldy, and as it was at night, she could not travel to Edinburgh.

"Sorry, did you say your name was Charlie?"

"Yes Mary I did, it is really Charles, but I get called Charlie by friends, so please call me that. After we have had this conversation, I would love to come to meet you in Kircaldy tomorrow if you are happy with that. It does not matter if it is the weekend or not, this is very important and we would like to get this man behind bars quickly. If you give me a brief description of what happened we can take it from there."

Mary went on to explain her experience with the Doc, and that she had saved Janice from him as well.

"Okay Charlie I would love to meet with you to-morrow, would it be at Kirkcaldy police station?" "That would be perfect Mary; I hope you will be okay with giving me your second name then. I will have a WPC attend our meeting and she will be on hand to take notes."

"Thank you Charlie, what time?"

"I would think ten-thirty would be suitable for me, how about you?"

"That's good, thank you."

Saturday morning at ten fifteen, CI Charles Blair arrives at St. Brycedale Road police station and he is welcomed by Sergeant Bill Taylor, who says to him,

"I have WPC Ann Andrews waiting for you in an interview room Sir. If you go right in I will stay here and wait on Mary arriving." CI Blair thanked him and suggested that if he could arrange a cup of tea, he would appreciate it.

"Not a problem sir."

When he met WPC Andrews in the room, he told her to call him Charlie, as this would help relax Mary when she was being questioned. "I will also call you Ann, if that is okay with you."

"Yes Sir, that is fine."

"Charlie, remember Ann, my name is Charlie."

She laughed and apologized to her boss.

Right on ten-thirty, Mary walked into the police station and met Sgt. Taylor, after she introduced herself to him; he escorted her to the interview room.

After he introduced Mary to the others, Charles asked Mary if she would kindly pass on her second name, she told him it was McCaferty, which Ann took note off.

He then thanked Mary and asked if she could give her story, right from the start.

Mary spent the next half-hour going over everything about that night, or as much as she recall.

She told him, that she could not remember anything of the actual assault, and she had no idea what had happened, or with whom. She just knew that because of the soreness in her body, she had been assaulted.

She said, "There is not much more I can tell you, other than the only thing that had stuck in my mind was the way he had pronounced the word 'about', it sounded more like aboot. It was only when I had heard his voice on TV, and it sounded similar, that I suspected that he could be the culprit. I took a picture and then drew a beard and moustache on it, and that was when I knew it was him."

Charlie asked her why she had decided to take matters into her own hands instead of contacting the police. Her answer did not surprise him as he had heard of these comments before.

She continued, "As it would have been my word

against a famous Doctor, I knew nobody would believe me, and he would get away with it, and that was why I decided to take matters into my own hands.

I started looking for him, and it took me a few months, but I eventually saw him in Dalkeith trying it on with Janice. When she had gone to the Ladies, I followed her and explained what had happened to me. She was delighted to help me get him, and agreed with me about nobody believing us, so we hatched a plan.

Charlie told Mary that even though she had thought that, she still should have told them, and now what I need to know is who is this Janice?

Mary told him she would only let him know if he promised that the two of them would not be prosecuted for attacking the doctor. She said that she was the one who had decided to do what they did, and there was no way she would put any blame on Janice.

Charles told Mary that he was a Chief Inspector and that he upheld the law, not enforce it, and that he could not guarantee that she would not be charged.

That was when Mary stood up, and said goodbye. CI Blair asked her to return and sit down, but she said back to him, "Only if you promise Charlie."

However, as there was no promise, she left the room. WPC Ann Andrews rose and ran after her, she asked Mary to wait a minute and think it over.

She told her that the police could charge her with

the assault on the Doctor if she did not comply, but Mary told her that until the Doctor came forward to complain they did not have a case, and they had no evidence without him.

"Like I said Ann, goodbye."

WPC Ann returned to the interview room and told her boss what Mary had said. Charlie could not believe that Mary had just done that. Bugger Ann, we needed her to catch this rapist, and without her, we could not charge him, even though we could find him. Can you get Chief Inspector Sutherland to come in Ann; I would like a chat with him. She told him, as he was out of the office at the present, that she would try to contact him.

When Mary returned home, she immediately telephoned Janice to bring her up to date with how the interview had gone. Janice thanked her for her loyalty, but she should have told the cops who she was. She said, "I could have told them that we should have cut his balls off at the time, which would definitely have stopped him attacking women again." Mary laughed and told her that was why I did not want to involve you Janice, we need to be very careful and get them to release us from any charges.

CHAPTER 17

The promenade. Kirkcaldy.
2006.

It is one week since Mary had the interview with CI Blair, and as it was a nice day she had decided to take a walk along the seafront; she is thinking that the fresh sea air could help her decide whether to go back to the police or not.

There was a spring tide that day, which meant that at low tide, the sea was further out than it would be on a Neap tide. A Spring tide means high highs and low lows, and in Kirkcaldy that meant the beach is very wide at this time.

She is enjoying watching a man throwing a stick into the water for his retriever dog to chase after, and return it to its master.

It is obvious to Mary that the dog is very playful and boisterous, so it must be quite young.

This time the man pretends to throw the stick and his dog begins to run into the water, then it realises that his master still has it in his hand. As the dog runs at him, it jumps up trying to get the stick, it knocks the man over and he falls backwards.

As Mary watches, she sees no sign of movement from him, so she immediately goes towards the steps down to the beach, and runs towards the man and his dog, which is licking at his masters' face. Because of the distance to the waters edge, it takes her a few minutes to get there.

As Mary approaches, the retriever is jumping around not sure of what has happened. She notices that the mans head had hit a rock, which was partly hidden in the sand. There was a lot of blood coming from his head, so she gets her mobile phone out and calls for emergency help. After explaining the situation, she was informed that police and the ambulance services were on their way, in addition, the air ambulance service had been called into action.

Within minutes, Mary could hear the sirens and she saw a police car arrive on the promenade, which was followed by an ambulance. The police and paramedics soon arrived at the scene and examined the man who was still unconscious. The tide had now turned and it was now very near to where he lay, which was a concern for the paramedics. As their patient could possibly have a broken neck, they did not want to take the chance of the long walk back to the ambulance. It was decided to get the air ambulance to land close to them and transfer their patient by air to the hospital.

As the helicopter approached, the pilot landed

about thirty-five meters from them. A paramedic ran from the chopper and he was informed as to the situation. He told the others that the pilot could not switch of the engines, so they would have to be careful as they approached the chopper. He explained that they could not switch the engine off because of the risk of the chopper sticking in the sand, especially if it did not start again.
The retriever was frightened by the helicopter and it had run a little distance away. As the paramedics were transferring their patient to the chopper Mary was trying to calm the pup down.

It very timidly came close to her and she managed to grab hold of its collar. She shouted to a police officer to see if the man had a leash on him, so he went to the chopper and asked the paramedics to have a look in his pockets for a leash for the dog. In addition, which hospital they were taking him to. Sure enough, the leash was there, and as they handed it over, they said that they would be heading to Edinburgh Royal. The officer took the leash to Mary who was still comforting the pup. They stayed where they were until the chopper had taken off, then the officer told Mary that he would appreciate it if she would go with him and the dog to St, Brycedale police station. With the dog obviously haven taking a liking to her she agreed to go with him.

On arrival at the police station, WPC Ann Andrews was standing at the desk and said hello Mary, have you come back to tell all. She told her

that she had not made her mind up yet, but said she was concerned about the man who had been injured on the beach, and what would happen to his dog. The officer that had come in with Mary, told her that the injured mans wife had been notified, and that she was on her way to pick up the puppy, which she would take home before heading to Edinburgh Royal to see her husband.
Mary said thank you, I think I will wait here until she arrives.

Fifteen minutes later, a woman walked into the police station and announced who she was. WPC Andrews told her that a woman called Mary McCaferty had seen what had happened and she was the one who called for help. She said the woman was waiting with the dog, to see her.

Mrs. Linda Errol walked into the room and introduced herself to Mary, and then, as the retriever was jumping with excitement to see her, she thanked her for helping her husband, and for taking care of Oscar. Mary asked her if she had heard how her husband was, and she said that he was in emergency and presently being treated for a head wound. He had been very lucky to have been rescued so quickly. Linda again thanked Mary and asked her for her phone number. She wrote her name and telephone number on a piece of paper and gave it to Linda, and asked her if she would call to let her know how her husband was.

"I most certainly will Mary, now I must hurry home with Oscar and head to Edinburgh to see

Larry."

They hugged each other and Mary patted Oscar, who gave her a big kiss.

About two weeks passed with no word on the man she had helped on the beach, she was wondering if he had possibly died, but surely, she would have been informed.

A month had passed when a knock came to her door; a police officer who was standing there, asked her if she was Mary McCaferty. Mary said that she was and then asked him what was wrong.

The officer smiled and asked if he could come in as he had good news for her.

Once inside and seated on her settee he told her that a Mr. and Mrs. Errol would like to see her, he was the man who you had helped rescue on the beach four weeks ago.

Mary breathed a sigh of relief when she heard this, and she asked the officer how he was.

He told her that he had recovered well and he is now recovering in his own home, after being released from the hospital two days ago. He said, "The Errol's want to thank you for saving his life and that is why I am here; they asked if a police officer could pick you up and take you to their home." "Why ask the police?" Mary said, "I only called the emergency services, nothing else."

He told her that it was a special request by a former Kirkcaldy Judge, and when they ask for something special, they get something special. As I am here now Ms McCaferty, perhaps if you can get ready I can take you to their home. They told me that they would like to see you tonight if possible. "Well yes I would like to see them and Oscar, he is a beautiful dog, so I will go get ready."

On the way to the Errol home, the two introduced each other by their first names, and Mary was thinking that he was quite nice looking, and she wouldn't mind a night with him.

She then told him that she only called for help, and caught the pup when the chopper arrived, nothing else. Ian Grant, the Officer, then explained to her that she had saved the Judges life. Because the tide had turned, it was coming in very fast at that part of the beach; Judge Errol would definitely have drowned if it had not been for you.

They soon arrived at the house and Mary was taken by surprise, it was a huge mansion on the outskirts of Kirkcaldy and within walking distance to the beach. There was a large Blue Jaguar car in the drive and another vehicle with the name of the local newspaper, The Fife Free Press, on the side.

"Oh God no, I hope they don't want to talk to me, said Mary."

Ian replied, "sorry, but I was told to say nothing about this, as you may not have come."
Mary laughed and called him a bugger then said,

"Oops sorry I should not be swearing at a police officer."

Ian smiled and said, "Its okay, but you may have to go on a date with me as a punishment."

"Happy to oblige officer, we can arrange it when you are taking me home."

Linda Errol gave them both a very warm welcome as she invited them in. Larry was in his chair next to a roaring log fire, but stayed seated when Mary approached him, he did apologise for not standing to greet her. She told him it was nice to see him looking a lot better than he had the last time she had seen him, and that she was happy to have helped him.

She was then introduced to a reporter from the newspaper, and a photographer, they were there to take a picture of Larry and Mary and write a story on what had happened that day. Mary's blush almost matched the colour of her hair as she was being asked to stand alongside Larry's chair. Then Oscar was brought into the room and after he calmed down from seeing Mary again, he too was photographed. Linda Errol had said that she did not want to be in the picture, even after Larry had told her that she should.

Linda said, "No matter who or what you were Larry, in this house it is my rules." Everyone laughed and Ian said, "That's you put in your place Judge."

She then told them that she was going to fetch tea for everyone, and then she left the room to let them to get on with talking to the press.

After all questions were asked, and answers given, Linda magically appeared with a tray, and the tea was served. As soon the press people left,

Larry told Mary that he and Linda wanted to reward her, she tried to say no but he continued.

"Linda and I had booked to see the musical Les Miserable's, in London's Sondheim Theater, in a couple of week's time. As I cannot go now, we have decided to present the tickets to you, and we had booked into the Thistle Hotel for three nights, which is only five minutes walk from the theater. I will transfer the room to your name Mary so that you can stay there." She replied by telling Larry that there was no way she could accept their offer even with the free tickets, she could not afford the trip. He went on to tell her that he had booked return flights from Edinburgh to London, and he would make sure that they were transferred to you as well. He said,

"We have already told the reporter about your reward, so you have no excuse Mary; all you have to tell me is who is going with you."
She thought for a minute and then said that she had a good friend Janice Dean. It was all agreed, and he said he would make sure that everything was put into place for the two of them, and the documents would be sent to her as soon as possible. Mary thanked them both.

After they had all made their goodbyes, including Oscar, she was back in the police car. Ian told her that he was off duty in two night's time, and asked her if she would go for dinner with him. The answer was a definite, yes.

CHAPTER 18

The Fife Free Press.

Mary could hardly wait to tell Janice what had happened that night, what with the reward and getting a date with a hunk of a police officer.
Janice thanked Mary for including her on the trip and to the musical; she said that it had been a wonderful offer from Larry Errol, however Mary you did save his life.

"I cannot wait to see the copper you lucky bugger, mind and let me know how the date goes."
She continued by asking Mary to take a picture of the newspaper report, as she did not get The Fife Free Press in Dalkeith, and send it to her.

"Will do Janice, I will call you tomorrow to hear what you think, It's a pity that Ian was not in the picture, but as it was not him that was at the scene, they decided not to put him in it."
"Well take one on your phone and send it to me as well. Talk tomorrow, Bye."

Monday morning came and as Mary was on her way to work, she popped into a shop to buy The Fife Free Press. The shopkeeper, Gladys, said hi, and typically of a local paper shop where gossip is rife, she continued to say what was in the report. Gladys told Mary that it was a very nice picture of her with the judge and his dog, and that she was famous now. She continued without stopping for breath and said,

"You have been introduced as a local heroine who is a qualified hairdresser and beautician, and it named the local shop where you worked. It was also reported that you had been rewarded with a trip to London, and that you were taking your best friend, Janice, with you."

Mary finally got a word in and she thanked Gladys, and almost said to her that she had no need to buy the paper now.

She left in a hurry, as she was due at her work in five minutes.

That day somewhere in a house in Fife, a certain person was reading the paper and came across the report and picture of Mary.

"Mary McCaferty you fucking bitch, I did say I would get you one day, and now that I know where you work, one way or another you are going to get it, and soon. I promise you that."

The next evening Mary was looking forward to her date, it was her first one for a few months.
Ian arrived dead on time, and as she answered the door, she said to him that she would be right out.
During their dinner date, Ian congratulated her on the beautiful picture in the newspaper, but said

that he was not surprised because she was beautiful. Everything was going well, when all of a sudden a woman came over to their table and began shouting at Mary's' date.

"Caught you at last you cheating bastard, I knew you must have been up to something, so I put a tracker on your car."

She took a ring from her finger and threw it onto the table saying,

"Fuck you Ian, you can forget our engagement, give that to your fucking bitch."

She turned and walked out of the restaurant. Mary was speechless for a few seconds then said to Ian, who was also obviously searching for words,

"Well I guess she got that one right, fuck you Ian, but thank you for the meal. One day you may regret double dating with me constable; nobody gets away with messing with a McCaferty. I will leave you to pay the bill, Goodbye."

She then rose from the table and walked out, leaving a few customers looking over to see what was happening to a very embarrassed Ian Grant.

Outside the restaurant, Mary saw Ian's ex fiancée and shouted to her.

"I did not know he was engaged, otherwise I would never have gone out with him."

"Its ok he has done it before, I let him off last time, but this is second time that I know off, so never again, your welcome to him."

She got into her car and drove off. Mary walked over to where a taxi was waiting on a fare; she stepped in and told the driver to take her to twenty five Denton Court.

On the way home she was thinking, my first date for months and he turned out to be a cheating bastard, will I ever find the right man?

When Mary arrived home the first thing she did after settling down, was to call Janice and tell her about the dinner date, Janice told her that it was good that she had found out about him before she had got into his bed.

Mary agreed, and said to her that she was now thinking about their trip to London, hoping that it will help her forget tonight.

"I am really looking forward to it as well Mary, and thank you again for including me. I will drive over to Kirkcaldy to pick you up, so that will save you catching a train to go to the airport, talk to you soon to make the arrangements."

"Thanks Janice, I appreciate that, love you, Bye."

Almost as soon as she had ended that call, her phone buzzed. She could see on the screen that it was Chief Inspector Blair.

"How can I help you Charlie?"

"Mary how about you and your friend Janice going into the police station in Kirkcaldy, and perhaps if we can all get together there we could help each other."

Mary replied,

"When we are sure that the Doctor can't charge us with assault, then and only then, we will talk

Charlie; have a good night Inspector, Bye."

CHAPTER 19

Edinburgh – London.

Edinburgh Airport is the sixth busiest airport in the United Kingdom; it is located in the Ingliston area, west of the city.

Nine-thirty am. Friday, May twenty sixth, and as promised, Janice picked Mary up at her home for the trip to Edinburgh airport, where their flights were booked with British Airways to London Heathrow. It was a nice and clear morning and the flight was on time. London here we come.

Once there the two took the Heathrow Express to Paddington station, where they then boarded a taxi to the Thistle Hotel.

After they booked in, the two women used the rest of Friday afternoon to set off on a shopping trip. Then on the Saturday morning, they took in a few of the sites, before going to the theater in the afternoon, where they were booked in for the two-thirty show.

After the show finished at five-twenty, Mary and Janice headed for a decent looking bar for a few drinks, before going back to their hotel. There was one not to far from the theater, and when they entered the bar it was very busy. Big Frank, one of the bouncers on the door said that the only two seats available was near a window where two men were already seated at the table.

Janice asked Mary what she thought about sitting there with them, and she quickly answered by saying to her that they would introduce themselves as a couple, that should put them off trying to chat us up.

They eased their way over through the crowd, and asked the men if they could sit at the table, one of them smiled and said that they would be happy to have their company. As soon as they sat down Mary leaned over, took hold of Janice's hand and said, "We were lucky to get a seat darling."

The two men laughed, then introduced themselves as Eric and Benny, Eric told the ladies that they were also a couple, that was when Mary also laughed and told them that she and Janice were not really a couple, we did not want you to come on to us.

Benny smiled and said there was no chance of that dear, you do not have the right parts. All four now laughed and began chatting as if they were old friends. Dirty jokes were passed back and forth, and stories told, then Eric said.

"There's that fucking creep just come in to the bar, you two are lucky to be with us or he would have been right over. He comes in often and trolls about looking to pick up women, I do not know why but there is something very strange about him, and I'm sure he wears a wig."

Mary and Janice were sitting with their back to the door but they both looked at each other at the same time and said, "No, it can't be him."
However, when they turned all the way round and looked, Mary said, "Shit, it is him."

Eric asked, "Don't tell me you two know him, I'm sorry if I offended you both."

Mary said, "Oh we know him alright, he date raped me and tried to do it to Janice."

"Yes and Mary saved me, and that's when we became best friends."

They went on to give the lads a brief description of what they had done to him. Both Eric and Benny had a good laugh at their description, and then Eric asked them if they wanted to get the police to him, Mary said, "I would rather see him run over by a bus."

"Well I can't arrange that ladies, but I can arrange a good hiding for him."

He told them that Big Frank and Mickey, over by the door, are the pub bouncers, so they can legally throw him out, and be a bit rough with it,

"What do you think?"

Janice and Mary looked at each other and nodded,

"Okay and if you can find a bus to run over him, better still," Mary laughed as she said it.

Eric beckoned to the two bouncers, and when they came over to their table, he introduced Mary and Janice to them. Then he briefly explained what the women had experience with the weirdo at the other side of the room. Frank, who was Scottish, said,

"We cannae hae that happen can we Mickey, especially tae lovely Scots lassies? C'mon lets go and hae a wee chat wi him."

Martin Symons was a bit shocked when the two bouncers approach him, and he asked what it was they wanted. Mickey told him to look across the room at the two women, who were now standing up and looking in his direction. Martin immediately recognised the two, but said that he had no idea who they were.

"Well they recognised you Mr. Symons, and they told me that you had a black dick, maybe we should go outside and have a look."

Frank added,

"And cut the fucker off so you Cannae dae it to another female."

Martin began to shake and panic; he knew he would be in trouble if he went out with these two big men. Pushing his way through some customers, he made a mad dash towards the door, with the bouncers on his tail.

As Mickey and Frank reached the door, only a few seconds after the doc, they heard a screech of brakes, and a thud. They could see that a taxi had hit Martin, and his body had fallen in front of it, ending up under its front wheels.

Mickey got his phone out and called the emergency services for an ambulance and the police. He waited at the scene for them, as big Frank went back inside to explain to the proprietor what happened. Frank told him that he and Mickey had spotted the man touching up a female customer who had slapped him, so they went after the man, he must have spotted us heading for him, and made for the door.

He said, "Unfortunately for the pervert, when he ran out into the road, there was a taxi passing by." The owner thanked Frank and told him that when the police come in to ask about the victim, he would explain why he had run out.

"You go and see to the two women you were chatting up Frank."

When he got to the table he apologized to Mary and Janice, "I am sorry ladies but we couldnae find a bus, however will a taxi dae?"

The two laughed and asked Frank if he was having a joke. He said to them, "The creep had run out onto the road and was hit by a passing taxi; he had ended up right under its wheels. I will be surprised if he recovers, and that's if he is not dead already."

Mary said, "Christ Frank, I was only kidding about the bus, but I will not lose any sleep over him, in fact I may sleep even better tonight."

Later when the police had finished interviewing all concerned, Mickey came back in and walked over to the table where the four friends were sitting. He told them that the paramedics had confirmed that the Doctor had died instantly. He said that he had overheard the police saying that the identification on the body had confirmed that the victim was a Doctor Martin Symons.

Mary, Janice, Eric and Benny all raised their glasses at the same time, and toasted, "Here's to karma."

Before the two couples parted for the evening, Mary and Janice promised to keep in touch with Eric and Benny, even though they all thought that it was highly unlikely that they would. As they left the bar, Mary handed Frank ten pounds and told the two men to have a drink on them. Both thanked the women and Frank said,

"Nice to have met you, have a safe night."

Sunday brought about a full day of more sight-seeing, but before they went out, Mary telephoned Chief Inspector Blair in Edinburgh, even though it was Sunday, she knew he would answer her call as soon as he saw her name pop up on his phone.

When he answered, he said, "Hi Mary, have you called to tell all at last?" She began by saying no, and then she explained about last night's incident as best she could to him, but left out the fact that she and Janice were instigators. All she said was, "The Doctor must have panicked when he saw the bouncers going for him because they had seen a woman slapping him. I did not realise who it was at the time, and only found out after the gossip started spreading round the bar. It was a shock to me Charlie, but as far as I am concerned, he deserved everything that he got."

The conversation, continued with questions and answers passing back and forward, and it lasted about half an hour, ending up with the CI asking Mary to get in touch with him as soon as she arrived back in Kirkcaldy.

Mary said, "Okay Charlie, now that I know he can't come after us, things have changed, I will see you soon, bye."

In Edinburgh, Charlie Blair is chatting with his wife and relaying what Mary had just told him.

"I do not know why Ashley, but I am worried about that one."

"What are you thinking dear?"

"It's okay I don't want to worry you with my problems."

"Well you know what they say Charlie, if you don't share your problems, I can't help you."

"Touché Ashley, I am sure there is something odd about her story, it just seems to be too much of a coincidence that she and Janice were in the same pub where the doctor was run down."

"Well you can call London tomorrow dear and find out what they have on report."

"Aye I know, but the fact that she called me makes me a wee bit suspicious of her side of the story. Bugger it, I am going to put that call in now, nothing ventured nothing gained."

He called into his police office in Edinburgh and

spoke to duty sergeant Davis, who under the CI's instructions, looked up the nearest office to the theater. He was taking a chance that the bar mentioned was close to where the show was, and so he contacted the nearest police station to there.

Within half an hour, the report was faxed through to Sgt. Lee Davis, who then sent it on to CI Blair.

After he had read it through, it was more or less exactly as Mary had told him. There was absolutely no mention of Mary and Janice in their report. He conveyed briefly, what the report said, to his wife and she told him,

"There you go Charlie; it was obviously just a coincidence that they were there, strange things do happen dear."

"Okay, but I am not completely convinced Ashley, there is something about Mary McCaferty that I don't quite understand, however I doubt if I will ever find out the truth."

Ashley said, "Charlie do you want me to go and let Gayle know about her husband?"

"Officially I have to be the one who does that love, but if you want to come with me I would appreciate it."

When Gayle Symons heard the news that her husband had died in an accident in London, she was not too upset about it and said,

"Maybe it was someone who had recognised him." Charles told her that there had been no arrests made, but it appears that he was running away from two bouncers in a bar, who had seen a woman slap him after he had inappropriately touched her.

Well that is the last I want to hear of him, other than my lawyer signing this house into my name. Charles and Ashley left a tearless Gayle to get on with her own life.

CHAPTER 20

Back to Scotland.

With the rest of the Sunday spent travelling round the city, the two women were well and truly knackered by the time they got back to their hotel. After a couple of drinks at the bar, they went to their room for a good nights sleep.

Monday morning found them on their British Airways flight back to Edinburgh, where they collected Janice's car from the short-term car park. The drive to Mary's home took them over the Forth Bridge into Fife, then along the A92 and on to twenty-five Denton Court, Kirkcaldy. Mary asked Janice if she wanted to go in for a cup of tea before heading home, but Janice told her that she was going straight home because she had things to sort out.

As she drove away, she did not notice, a little down the street, another vehicle had moved away from the kerbside. It followed her at a reasonable distance, back over the Forth Bridge and onto the Edinburgh bypass, all the way to Janice's' home in Dalkeith.

The person following slowed down, as Janice drove into a driveway, and then eased their car just past the drive and stopped. Janice by this time had picked up her case and was entering her house. She was excited to be home and did not notice the stranger leave the vehicle and walk up towards her door.

Standing in her front room Janice heard a noise behind her, and turned around. "Who are you and why are you in my home?"

"I've come to get revenge on fucking Mary McCaferty, if I can't have her, she's not getting you either."

"What the hell are you talking about; Mary and I are like sisters."

It was then that Janice noticed the stranger pull out a large knife, she made a grab for it, but the blade slashed her hand as the stranger pulled it back. "You're a fucking lying bitch, I know you spent the weekend with her, take that."

The knife was plunged into Janice's chest. Then it was pulled free as Janice fell to the floor with her unbelieving eyes staring at the attacker.

Just then, a voice was heard from the front door, "Hi Janice its Babs from next door, I saw that you were home so I had to come round and see how your trip to London went."

The attacker hid behind the living room door and shouted come in Babs. As she entered the room, she was about to ask Janice if she liked the show, when she saw her laying face down on the floor, suddenly she felt a pain in her back. She half twisted round as she was falling to the floor and the attacker lost grip on the weapon. Panic now set in, so it was get the hell out of here as fast as I can.

Barbara's husband Norman saw a person run from the house next door, and jump into a car parked in the street. He wondered if something was wrong, so he headed over to Janice's home.

The door was open so he stepped inside shouting,

"Everything okay in here," then he saw Barbara lying on the floor with a knife sticking out of her back and Janice just a few feet away laying in a pool of blood. In a state of shock, he knelt down to see if his wife was still alive, and as he did so he took his phone from his pocket and dialed the emergency services.

Paramedics and police were on the scene within a few minutes, and a Police Sergeant told Norman it would be best if they went back to his house.

He did not want to leave his wife, however the officer convinced him that it was best to leave it to the paramedics to get on with their jobs. Sergeant Dean Dayton and a WPC walked next door with him.

Once there, the Sergeant asked Norman what had happened.

He said, "I knew Babs had noticed that Janice had got home, so she had gone over to see her. I was cleaning the inside of our living room windows when I saw a woman run from the house, jump into a car, and drive off at speed. I thought it was strange, so I headed over to find out. That was when I saw my wife on the floor, with a knife in her back, and then Janice laying next to her."

"Wait a minute, you say you saw a woman run from the house Norman, can you describe what she looked like, and did you notice what make of vehicle she was in?"

"She had a pair of jeans on, and what looked like a black leather jacket."

"Are you sure it was a woman Norman?"

"Oh yes she had long hair and a huge bust that bounced as she ran to her car, it was definitely a woman Sergeant."

"What about the car?"

"It was a blue Ford Focus and the registration number was AB52 BRE that I am sure about sir, with the BRE reminding me of her big breasts."

The Sergeant gave a little smile and then said, "Wow, well done Norman, with that information, you have provided, if the vehicle is not a stolen, I am sure we can find the attacker. He told the WPC to get that number put through to the office and find out the owner and address.

She headed out of the house and called the vehicle number in, within a couple of minutes the station came back with the result. She went back inside and handed the note to sergeant Dayton, who thanked her.

"Okay Norman, do you know anyone from Kirkcaldy."

"Yes Sergeant our neighbour Janice was with her good friend Mary McCaferty on a trip to London over the weekend, she comes from Kirkcaldy, but I don't think she has a car."

"That was not the name we came up with Mr. Smith, but thank you anyway, you have been very helpful. Just then, another officer entered and told them that the ambulance was ready to leave with Mrs. Smith. The paramedics are waiting on her husband to go with her. Sergeant Dayton told Norman to grab his jacket and go, he would make sure the house was secured, and that he would get an officer to take the key to the hospital for him. Norman did not need to be told twice, and as he was going out, he thanked the Sergeant.

When he was back in his Dalkeith police office, Sergeant Dayton was reporting to his Chief Inspector and relaying to him that they were in the process of contacting Kirkcaldy. He said, "Mr. Smith told me that Janice Dean knew a Mary McCaferty from there, but the owner of the vehicle number came back as a Brenda Gray from Kirkcaldy. I was wondering if there is a possible connection between this Gray and McCaferty women.

After I contacted Sergeant Bill Taylor in Kirkcaldy, he told me that he did not know of a Brenda Gray, but that Mary McCaferty was well known to him, in fact, he was waiting to hear from her regarding another case. He also informed me that she had recently saved the life of a former local Judge. He told me that he would send out a car to see if this Brenda Gray was at home, and if not he put out an APB for the vehicle." Sergeant Taylor also said that he personally would be speaking to Ms McCaferty, and then get back to us. We did tell him that Janice Dean, Ms McCaferty's' friend, had died at the scene, and to be careful, just in case there was a connection between her and the suspect.

Denton Court, Kirkcaldy.

Sergeant Bill Taylor accompanied by WPC Ann Andrews, knocks on the door of number twenty-five. Mary hears the knock, and as she opens the door, she is taken by surprise to see the police standing there,

"Hello Sergeant, I did not expect to see you as soon as this, what can I do for you?"

"Can we come in Mary; I have some news for you." The news he had for her was definitely not what she had expected. Tears were running down her face as she said,

"I can't believe that Janice is dead, no way Sergeant. She just left me a short time ago."

He went on to explain briefly what had happened, and then asked her if she knew a Brenda Gray.

"What's that cow got to do with this, are you saying that she is involved?"

WPC Andrews asked Mary how she knew Ms Gray, and she replied that she used to live with her; however, she left out the part that she slept with Brenda Gray.

The WPC told Mary that it was Ms Gray's car that was seen at the address, and then asked her what kind of relationship the two had. Mary told her that when she left, Brenda was not happy and she had said that she would get me back one day. She was gay, and she was very jealous that I was seeing a man; she wanted me and only me in her bed. The WPC asked, "And did you."

"That is my private business."

"Well it may lead to some kind of revenge by her Mary, so it is our business as well, so did you?"
"If you must know I did on a couple of occasions, only because she let me live there. It was because I was homeless at the time, and I had nowhere else to go."

WPC Andrews told her that Brenda Gray might have something to do with the attack in Dalkeith; and if so, perhaps you should be very careful until the police find her.

"Bloody hell, you don't think that she killed Janice?"

"It is a strong possibility Mary."
Sgt. Taylor then mentioned the death of Doctor Martin Symons. Mary told him that she had already chatted with a Chief Inspector Charles Blair from Edinburgh, about what had happened in London, and that she had promised to talk more about it later.

Just before they left, the Sergeant and WPC Andrews, told her again to be very careful, and that they would be in touch when they find Brenda

Gray.

When the police arrived at the home of Brenda Gray, she appeared to be very intoxicated, and when they asked her about what she was doing in Dalkeith earlier in the day, she told them she could not remember where she had been.

She was told that she was being arrested and charged with one count of murder, and another one of attempted murder.

Brenda started to protest, but one of the officers asked about a red mark on the sleeve of her jersey.

"Oh I spilt some jam on it," she said.

"Well we will see exactly what it is once we get it checked at the station." He then handcuffed her and the two officers escorted her to their car.

Later at the police station, Sgt Taylor called Mary to inform her that they had arrested Brenda Gray. He told her that she had been charged, and will be remanded in custody until she appears in court, so you will not have to worry about her coming after you Mary.

"Thank you sergeant I appreciate your call."

CHAPTER 21

Mary tells Inspector Jim
Scappa where to go.

Two days later, Mary arranged to meet with Inspector Jim Scappa at Kirkcaldy police station. When they had met previously he had told her to call him Jim, so when she went into his office she said.

"Hi Jimmy how are you, we really have to stop meeting so often, people will start to talk about us." The Inspector laughed at her wee joke, and then began with his questions.

"Okay Mary, I want to know the truth about what went on in London, it seems to me that it was far too much of a coincidence that you and your friend Janice were in that same pub as Doctor Symons. I want to know how you found out he would be there, and did you and Janice pay the two bouncers to throw him in front of the taxi?"
Mary burst out laughing,

"I can't believe that you would think of me as an accomplice to having the Doc killed Jimmy that is the most ridiculous thing I have ever heard."

She went on to tell him that it was a pure coincidence, and that she and Janice were there with two men friends. She told him that she even had their names and contact numbers if he did not believe her, you can call them now if you like.
All the time knowing that the men would back up her story completely. The Inspector asked her for the contact details and she took the paper with the numbers on it, out of her handbag, and threw it across the table at Jim, who told her to wait there. Mary shouted,
"Fuck you Jimmy; if you do not believe me, then I am not waiting here." Then, as she walked out of his office, she showed him a single finger salute and told him not to mess with a McCaferty. The Inspector could not believe what had just happened in his office, but he also knew that he could not stop her unless he arrested her, and he could not do that without proof. However, he decided to call the numbers she had given him, just in case.
The answers from both men were not what he wanted to hear, they matched Mary's story in every detail.
An annoyed Inspector Scappa was not having a good day, he is saying to himself, she has went from hero to villain in a matter of weeks, and getting away with it, bloody Mary McCaferty.

When he got home that night, he was not in a good mood, and Jan, his wife, asked him what was wrong.

"It's that bloody Mary McCaferty dear, she had the cheek to tell me to fuck off today, and in my own office at that. Then she stuck a finger up at me as she walked out."

Jan started laughing at him and said,

"I have even thought about doing that to you before James."

He smiled back to her and said, "That's what I love about you dear, you are not bitchy enough, unlike Mary bloody McCaferty. I will be glad when next year comes, and I can retire from all the stress."

Jan still laughing said,

"Perhaps having you around the house all day long, I will be the stressed and bitchy one, watch out for that finger dear."

TEN WEEKS LATER.

In Denton Court, Mary has not long arrived home from her work, and she is having a shower, when her doorbell rings. Bugger she thinks why now. She steps out of the shower, wraps a towel round her head, tying her long red hair up. Then she puts on her dressing gown. By this time, the doorbell is ringing again, and she shouts.

"I'm on my way,"
On opening the door there is a tall handsome man standing there, he asks.

"Are you Mary McCaferty?"

"Why, who are you, and what do you want?"

"My name is Norman Smith; we lived next door to your friend Janice Dean, and Barbara, my wife was the other victim of the stabbing."
Mary told him she was so sorry and asked him to come inside, she joked,

"It's not every day that I have a handsome man at my door."
He replied,

"And its not every day I arrive at the door of a half dressed beautiful woman."

Once inside Mary told him to sit down and she would make them a cup of tea, then you can tell me your news. As she was making the tea, she was thinking to herself that if she played her cards right she could have him tonight.

When she came back with the tea, and as she laid the tray down on a coffee table in front of the settee, she made sure that he could see her bare chest down the front of her dressing gown.

Mary then sat down next to Norman, who could not help noticing that her dressing gown had opened up a little, revealing her long legs.

"Well what is the good news you have for me Norman?"

He went on to explain that Janice's father, James, had decided to present her with Janice's gold wrist-watch. She had told him how good a friend you had been and that you were the one who had saved her from being raped.

"Wow I never expected that."

As she leaned over to take the watch from him, the top of her dressing gown slid off her shoulder.

"Oops sorry Norman," and she pulled it back up. However, Norman had already had a good eyeful of her breasts and he was feeling a little turned on. Mary recognised the signs, and as she had a quick look at his crutch, she noticed a certain bulge. She asked Norman,

"How is your wife? It must be difficult for you both."

"Yes it is Mary; she has been home for two months now, but she still does not want to lie on her back yet. Sex is out of the question because she is scared that I hurt her, so it does get a bit frustrating. I just have to be patient with her as she has had a terrible experience. However it does cause a friction between us at times and we start arguing."

"I know how that goes Norman; I have not had a boyfriend for months now, it does get frustrating." Mary decided to make a move on him and placed a hand high up on his thigh, then she leaned over a little, making sure that the top of her dressing gown fell down again. Norman reminded her that he was a married man, and it would not be right. Mary said,

"I will not tell if you don't, I can tell that you are excited at seeing my tits Norman, why don't you have a feel of them." She pushed her chest out and he could not resist, when he did, she began to unzip his trousers, and slipped her hand inside. Norman was now the fly caught in Mary's web, there was no way he could escape. Mary's bed was their next stop.

Later as he was leaving Mary's home, she kissed him on the cheek and thanked him for bringing the watch. He started to say that the sex should never have happened, but Mary interrupted him by saying,

"I know you enjoyed it as much as I did Norman, and if you are ever back in this area again, please look me up." He smiled and said,
"You never know Mary, you never know, Bye."

EDINBURGH 2007.

Mary is in the city with some female friends who are on a girl's night out, and as they are enjoying the evening, Mary spots Tom Bates in the same bar. Tom was with a female and had not noticed Mary, however as soon as she saw him she remembered Tom calling her a devious bastard.

Hmm she thought I wonder what I can do to get my own back on him. Then an idea struck her and she started to tell her friends about him, and what he had called her, two years previously. Then she asked them if they would help her get back at him.

"What have you got in mind Mary?" said one of them.

She told them of her thoughts and the women were all for it.

One of the women, Helen, walked over to where he was sitting and slapped him across the face, as she did so, she shouted. "You fucking bastard Tom, I should have got the police to you for raping me." Then she told the woman who was with him that she would be better getting as far away from him as possible. Helen was smiling as she walked back to her friends, and as she did so, Tom was trying to say that he had never seen her before, however the woman with Tom stood up and shouted, fucking pervert, and then walked out of the bar.

Then Mary and two of the other women went over to an embarrassed Tom, and started shouting at him, "Pervert, pervert, pervert."

It was then that Tom noticed Mary was one of them, and as he was about to try to hit her, two pub bouncers grabbed him, as they threw him out of the door, they told him he was barred.

Within seconds another man walked over to the women's table and said, "Hello Mary, nice to see you again," it was Norman Smith.

"What was all that about with that man Mary?"

"Oh hi Norman, that was a man that had called me a devious bastard, and nobody says that to me and gets away with it."

"Well I'm glad that we parted as good friends Mary."

"What are you doing here on your own Norman, where is your wife?"

"Barbara is over at a table in the corner Mary, I just noticed you because of all the shouting going on. She has been doing well since I last saw you; she says that when I went to see you about the watch you must have said something to me that changed my attitude." With that said, he gave her a wink.

Mary smiled and said to him that she was glad her therapy had worked, and they both laughed.

Helen said,

"I did not know you were a therapist Mary."

"I will tell you all about it later Helen, but I must go over and see Barbara; I'll be back in a minute."

Barbara had not met Mary before, and as soon as Norman had introduced her, she joked.
"Norman, I'm surprised that you came back to me after meeting this beautiful woman."
Norman blushed slightly and said to her in a joking context,
"I was tempted darling."
Little did his wife know that the therapy was sex.
Barbara continued,
"Well whatever you said to him Mary, it worked; he was a different man when he came home. I should thank you for saving our marriage."
"It was my pleasure Barbara, I am so glad to have helped." As she said that, she gave Norman a great big smile.
Before Mary left their table, Barbara told her that if she was ever in Dalkeith she should look them up. Mary told her she would be happy too, she said, "it was nice to meet you Barbara, Bye.

As soon as Mary returned to her friends, Helen asked her what Norman had meant when he said you were a good therapist.
After she explained what had happened, Helen said, "You are a right bastard Mary, shagging a married man, however after seeing him, I would have done the same." All the other women had a good laugh and said, "So would they."

Meanwhile, over at Normans table, Barbara was asking him exactly what Mary had said to him that had made him a lot less stressed when he had came home. Then she asked him, "Did you shag her?"
So as not to show his embarrassment, Norman did not know where to look,
"You shit Norman, I bet you did," Then she surprised him by saying, "I shouldn't really blame you, I was a right bitch to you when I was ill.
She is so beautiful. At least she saved our marriage, and I am thankful for that. I forgive you darling. I think we should go home and you can make love to me the way you did to her."

Norman, breathing a huge sigh of relief, smiled and said, "Let's go sweetheart."

As they left the bar, Barbara walked past the table with all the women at it, and said,

"Norman told me what had happened Mary, I am not angry at you, in fact the opposite. We are off home now, and I am sure he will be thinking of you when he is making love to me tonight. As long as it makes him really hard, I will enjoy it for the first time in months."
With that said, the two left the bar.

Mary's friends could hardly believe what they had just heard and Helen said, "I should rephrase what I said a while ago, you are one lucky bastard Mary, many a wife would have smacked you one.
We will have to call you Mary McCaferty, Therapist. From now on." All the friends laughed.

CHAPTER 22

2010.

It is a special year for Mary; she will be turning thirty in July and had not had a male friend for a couple of years. I must be losing my touch she is thinking. Maybe I should try a holiday and possibly meet a nice man, but where to go that is the question. The problem with that is it would be a distant relationship.

What Mary did not realize was that, approaching her flat at that moment were three men who had got together to get their own back on her. They were the three students who Mary had tricked into attacking her on her twenty-second birthday. All three had been sent to prison for three and a half years each, and now in their late twenties they wanted revenge.

When she heard the knock at her door, she first checked the spy hole in the door and as she did not recognise the young bearded man standing there, she called out and asked what he wanted. The man said that he was from Kirkcaldy police and he had an invitation for her, it was regarding a Sergeant Bill Taylor's retirement party. As soon as she opened the door, the man pushed Mary back into the room, and another two men followed him in.

"Its pay back time McCaferty," said Oliver, the first man, "we spent years in jail because of you, you fucking bitch."

Before she could do or say anything Liam and Noah had grabbed her, and as they held her, Oliver placed tape over her mouth. Mary was helpless against the three strong men, and soon she was stripped naked, thrown onto her bed, and each man then taking it in turns to rape her.

Before they left her flat, Oliver told her that if she told the police, they would make sure that her brother would die a horrible death.

"You understand what I have just told you bitch," he said.

A tearful Mary nodded to him, all the time thinking, I will kill you lot first you bastards.

It took Mary a few days to settle down and begin to gather her thoughts on how to get back at them.

Helen, one of the women who was in her group of friends, received the call from Mary.

"I need help Helen, can you get the others together and come round to my place on Friday night, I have something to talk to you all about.

When that night came, Mary informed the group

of her experience, and they all agreed that they should get together and sort the men out, but how? Sonja, the wild one of the group suggested that they should trap them and cut their balls off. "Not a bad idea said Helen, but we need to be sure that they cannot come back at Mary."

Tracy said

"I think we should kill those fuckers."
Mandy then said that she had an idea, and the others agreed with her.

Mary said, "That's it then, we are all agreed, let's do it." The women set out the plan.

Four weeks later Oliver, Liam and Noah had separate dates, and unknown to each one, the women all knew each other.

During the evening, each man had been invited back to his dates flat; however, what they did not know was that they would all be in the same flat.

The women had pre-arranged that the men would arrive at different times, and when Noah, the first one to arrive, was surprised to see another five women there.

Before he knew it, he was grabbed by them, then tied and tape put over his mouth.

Liam was next and Oliver soon followed him. Once all three were lined up, they were stripped naked and their arms were then taped to a chair each. They were told that if they tried to struggle, their balls would be cut off.

Judy produced her tattoo gear and began on Noah

first; there was no chance of doing anything to the penis of each man, as there was not enough space on the shrunken exhibit of the frightened men.

It took until nearly three in the morning when Judy had finished all three men, but they now all had the same thing done to them.

On all six arms, she had tattooed 'My prick is 2 inches long,' with the same on each mans back. Then after they had had their pubic hair shaved, she had tattooed the word 'useless' with an arrow pointing down to the penis.

The men were left tied up until six the next morning, and they were taken by surprise when Mary McCaferty arrived at the apartment.

She stood in front of the men and told them that this was what happens when you fuck with a McCaferty.

"Now if you ever even think about revenge, we will not only take it out on you, but your parents as well. You understand?"

All three nodded at the same time. Next, the naked men were made to drink as much alcohol as possible, and soon, a few other men, who were friends of the women, arrived and they blindfolded Noah, Oliver and Liam, then they were marched outside and into the back of a van.

When they reached their destination, the blindfolds, and gags were removed and the three were then tied to each other, and to the gates at the entrance to a public park.

An anonymous call went into the local police station, stating that three naked drunken louts were carrying on at the park.

Police soon arrived and all three were arrested once more. The officers in attendance took statements, however, as there were no witnesses, they took them to the police station and locked them up until the were sober.

When they appeared in court, it was revealed that they had been in trouble for rape a few years back. The judge decided that these three men had possibly been trying it again, and they had been punished when friends of the victim caught them.

He sentenced each one to three months in prison, and they were warned not to go near the park again.

Even though they had said that a Mary McCaferty had been the instigator, the Judge told them that she had had a perfectly good alibi, and that they obviously had it in for her because it was she, they had tried to rape a few years ago.

Mary and a few of her friends were in court to witness the decision and clapped as the men were led away.

As Mary had been through a horrible rape by the three men, she decided to give men a miss for a long time.

CHAPTER 23

2013.

After the hairdressers Mary worked with, was taken over by new owners, she remained on the books, but only in a part time basis. However, it meant that she had to give up her flat in Denton Court.

She is now living with her brother Gerry at Denton Road Kirkcaldy.

Gerry, who is a van driver, is working for Frank Muir. He collects packages from Frank twice a week and distributes them to his clients all round the County of Fife.

Gerry never mentions to Mary that he is running drugs for Frank, however she is not stupid, and as long as he gave her a roof over her head she was happy.

Well almost happy, sleeping on a couch in his one bedroom flat was not ideal for a thirty three year old woman.

On one afternoon when she was in the shop

working, a sales rep from one of their suppliers came in, and he asked to see her boss. Mary told him that she was at the accountants and would not be back for some time.

Steve Kirk was a bit of a flirt every time he came in, and this time was no different. He was all over Mary, who liked the attention but not the man.

Steve eventually asked Mary to go out for dinner after she finished her work, he told her about a very nice place near Anstruther. Mary not really wanting to accept, but also did not want to miss out on a free dinner, said that she would go on condition that she did not want it to be at the famous fish and chip shop there.

Steve laughed and told her it was The Craw's Nest Hotel, in Pittenweem. He told her that he would book a table for them and pick her up at her home about seven o'clock. Mary said to him,
"One more condition, no overnight stay."
Steve replied,
"That is a shame, but okay Mary if you say so."

All the time he was hoping to land up in her bed for the night. Little did Steve know that Mary slept on a sofa in her brother's home, and he had no chance anyway.

The drive to Anstruther, which was about forty-five minutes along the winding East Fife coast road, took them about fifty minutes.

The table reserved for them was next to a window and they had a wonderful view over the Forth Estuary.

After their meal, Steve did mention about a room for the night but the look he got from Mary told him that there was no way that was going to happen. Ah well it was worth a try he thought.

On the drive back along the coastal road, Steve was trying to play it cool with Mary, and the winding road meant that he had to keep both hands on the steering wheel.

By the time they reached Cameron Bridge, the next part of the A 915 road is called the Standing Stane Road. It is a long and reasonably straight one, which runs between Cameron Bridge and Kirkcaldy.

As drivers were impatient after many miles of being stuck behind slower vehicles on the coastal road, chances were often taken. Because of that, it is well known for the number of accidents on it.

Steve thought that he could now chance putting his hand on Mary's knee and as he did so, a red mini with four young men inside, decided to pass them. They had noticed that the driver of the car in front of them was looking at his passenger more than the road.

As they were passing, the mini driver peeped the horn and all three passengers were giving Steve the finger.

Suddenly, coming in the opposite direction, another vehicle appeared in front of the mini.

The mini driver, with his attention on Steve's car, noticed the other vehicle at the last minute. As he swerved to avoid it, he collided into Steve's car, which then mounted the grass verge and smashed through an old rusty fence.

Unlucky for Steve there were many trees in that area and he hit one square on. Mary could only watch as shards of glass, that looked like very small ice cubes, were flying towards her face in slow motion. Just as they hit her, the airbag burst open and saved her from serious injury. It seemed like it had all happened in slow motion, but in fact it was all over in a couple of seconds.

As the bag deflated, Mary noticed that Steve was pulling at his legs, and he was saying that they were trapped.

"Help me Mary." He shouted.

"I'm saving myself Steve, fuck you."

She released her seatbelt and tried to open her door, but it would not move, so she decided to climb through the broken window of the door. Steve was still shouting at her to help him; however, she was more concerned for herself and went about trying to climb through the window.

While all this was happening, the red mini car, although damaged in the collision, had kept going. The driver had obviously realised that he was in the wrong.

The vehicle that had come towards them, had also kept going, they too did not want to stop, for whatever reason they had.

A white transit van had been a little behind the mini when it had begun to overtake Steve. As it arrived on the scene, the driver noticed a female struggling to climb out of the side window of the crashed car, so he ran over to help her. He heard the male driver shouting for help, and he shouted back to him,

"After I get the woman out."

Just as he freed Mary from the car, the engine burst into flames, he half picked up, half pulled at Mary, to get her as far away as possible from the now flaming wreck.

They both heard the screams from Steve, but as the flames were fierce; the van driver could not get near enough to help him.

Steve's car was engulfed in flames and the trees were now afire as well. There was no way anyone could help the now silent Steve.

Fire crews, ambulance and police were on the scene very quickly; they had often been called out to accidents on this road and they were well experienced with problems in this area. The road was immediately sealed off to all vehicles, other than the emergency ones.

Mary was shaking with fright, and between the flying glass, and her climbing out through the broken window, her face and arms were covered in cuts and bruises. After being treated at the scene by the paramedics, she was eventually taken by ambulance to the Victoria hospital Kirkcaldy. Before they left the scene, she had managed to give the police her brother's information and phone number.

When they called him, he was informed that his

sister Mary had been involved in a serious accident on the Standing Stane Road. Gerry asked if she was okay, and he was informed that she had been injured but not life threatening, they also told him that she was on her way to the Victoria Hospital.

Gerry's first thought was to get to the hospital as soon as possible.

At the hospital, Mary was treated for the minor cuts to her face, arms and legs, which were injured as she was being helped out of the car.

When she was informed that Steve Kirk had not made it from the vehicle she broke into tears, more for thinking that it could have been her and not him that had been trapped and burned to death.

Gerry took his sister home and told her, as she was suffering from shock, to use his bed for a few days. He would be the one sleeping on the couch for the time being.

CHAPTER 24

Frank Muir.

Mary had been living with Gerry for about six months, when one day a young man called Billy Booth arrived to see Gerry.

Before long, twenty seven year old Billy is asking Mary to have dinner with him.

Even although he was six years younger than she was, she agreed to go out with him, after all, it would mean a free meal.

During the dinner, they were talking about Mary staying with her brother and having to sleep on his couch. Billy said to her that he had a small spare room in his flat, and if she was prepared to do the housework and make his meals for him, she could live there rent-free, and she could move in right away if she wanted too. Mary thought for a second or two then said ok.

Billy also worked for Frank Muir and his job was to go to Glasgow to collect the packages for him.

After a couple of weeks, Billy and Mary had been drinking, and Mary said to him that she was not wanting to sleep in that little room again, so she grabbed Billy's arm and took him into his room. Sex with him was over in a couple of minutes, which left Mary frustrated, but at least I have a bed and a free roof over my head, she said to herself.

About three months later, Billy had a visitor; it was his boss Frank Muir. Mary and six foot two Frank had an instant attraction to each other, which went unnoticed by Billy who was counting his wages at the time.

Two days later Frank arrived at the flat, and Mary said to him that Billy was away to Glasgow. He replied,

"Aye I know Mary, it was me that sent him there, it is you I am here to see, not Billy."

He took her in his arms and kissed her as she had not been kissed for a long time. Next thing she knew was that Frank picked her up and carried her into Billy's bedroom. Big Frank Muir certainly lived up to his name.

This was to be a regular meeting between the two, and by coincidence, it just so happened, when Billy was away to Glasgow.

Mary continued living with her boyfriend Billy Booth, but every week or so, she is in bed with Frank Muir, and enjoying him on top of her. Frank was thirty-eight years old. Mary at thirty-four years old, liked older men, and sex was always wonderful with Frank.

She had always said that they were much nicer to women. All the younger men she had been with were only interested in satisfying themselves, it was just a case if wham, bam, thank you ma'am, with them. Older men were so much better in bed. They tended to take their time in foreplay and they made sure that the women were satisfied as well as themselves.

On one occasion, after making love for twenty minutes with Frank, she says, as they lay back resting,
 "Billy will be home soon Frankie, maybe it is time for you to leave."
"I'm not finished yet lass, one more quickie, and then I'm off," whispers Frank.
"We sure don't want Billy to find you with me, and in his bed. You know he's not right in the head, he goes really crazy when he loses his temper."
"Aye lass but you need me too give you a good seeing too now and then, I know that he can't keep you happy. In a few minutes I'll just pop out for a pint and come back after he gets home."
Frank turns onto his side and begins to fondle Mary's breasts; soon they are at it again.
After he finishes his quickie with Mary, he puts his clothes back on, and as he heads out the door, he says to her, "see you in a wee while love."

Twenty eight year old Billy had been in Glasgow handing over a well-sealed envelope and picking up Franks packages from the suppliers. He was now returning them to Frank in Kirkcaldy. As he is driving home, he is thinking over things that the Glasgow mob had been saying to him, and he is wondering why Mary is still with him.

She often says that I fail to satisfy her when we have sex. Huh, just because she is getting old it is not my fault that she cannot enjoy a good bunk-up. I guess it must be the money and the free room and board I give her. At least I get satisfied, he says to himself, so it is worth keeping her there.
Little does he know, at that same time as he was thinking that, Frank was shagging Mary in his bed.

As Billy arrives back in his ground floor flat at Briarwood Lane, he asks if Frank has been in touch.
"Never seen him," says Mary without blushing,
"Were you expecting him today?"
"Aye, I was lass, and I do need to see him, I certainly hope he will not be too long?"
A little later Frank arrives at the flat, and winks as he says hi to Mary. Then he and Billy settle down to discussing the 'business' over a can of beer each. The packages are passed over to Frank, and money exchanged for Billy's wages. Frank then says his goodbyes, and heads out the door with another wink to Mary, as he leaves with a big satisfied grin on his face.

That night, Billy and Mary lie in bed after another failed attempt to satisfy her. Not surprising, she thinks, as she had already been well and truly satisfied earlier that day by Frank.

Mary soon falls asleep and Billy is again beginning to ponder on some of the things the drug suppliers had said to him about Mary. There was always a little snigger, when Frank's name was mentioned in conversation. What did they mean?

After a semi sleepless night, Billy's thoughts were that he really must look into what they were talking about and laughing at.

Was there something going on with Frank and Mary? No, surely not, somebody would have seen something and told me by now, he thinks.

CHAPTER 25

Gerry's surprise.

Frank wakes up at seven am, rises, showers, has his corn flakes, and heads out for a special business day. However, that something special on his mind today, is that he suspects, one of his contacts is cheating on him by using a cutting agent to his supply of drugs. The suspect is Gerry McCaferty.

This would not be good, as word would soon get around, that he was supplying poor drugs. They would start going elsewhere, or even taking it out on him, not a good thing to happen.

He meets Gerry at their normal meeting point, at the far corner of the Asda car park, and passed over the goods. Frank acted like there was nothing different from the usual hand over.

Gerry McCaferty had no idea that Frank had suspected him of cutting the drugs, however, as he knew about Frank having it off with Mary, his sister, he thought that he would be safe. This had led him to be a little bit careless.

After he had passed the packages on to Gerry in the morning, Frank went about his normal day and getting some shopping done.

That evening, he set about putting his plan into action; he is hiding in a nearby close and waiting for Gerry to go on his delivery rounds. He follows him to each of the drop off points, during which, he noticed that there was one extra point that he did not know about. After the round was complete, and with Frank's count of the packets that Gerry sold on, there was one extra package. He was now sure of his suspicions; Very soon, Gerry was due for a wee surprise.

Big John Williams, is a forty year old ex coal miner originally from Wales, and his best and only pal, Alan Deans, age forty five, is an ex forestry worker, from Ullapool, on the North West coast of Scotland. The two now reside in Livingston, near Edinburgh. With a population of fifty-seven thousand, it is the largest town in West Lothian.

John lived in a house at twenty-five Brandwell Lane and Alan in flat 12d, at forty–four Queens Street.

The two men had the reputation as being the hard men, of the town.

Through the grape vine, Frank heard of the two, and he arranged a meeting. After they introduced each other, and the normal conversation about the weather conditions talked about, Frank then got down to business.

He detailed what he wanted from the two, and then offered both of them a hundred and fifty pounds each, half now and half on completion of the assault, when and if they carried it out to his full instructions. The two agreed to do the deed, but wanted three hundred each; Frank knew that they would want to barter, so he offered two hundred and twenty five pounds. They came back with two seventy-five and Frank said he would settle for two hundred and fifty pounds each, no more. That sum was agreed, and they said that the deed would be carried out within the next couple of weeks.

Ten days later, in an alley just off Main Street, Kirkcaldy, a police constable who was on duty in that part of the town, came across what at first appeared to be a down and out drunk sleeping in a dark doorway. However, he soon realised that there was a bag over his head and not a jacket, and there was a large amount of blood lying around the body.

On closer inspection, he realised that it was a seriously beaten up body of a man. The call went in to the local emergency services and an ambulance arrived at the scene just after another couple of cops had arrived.

It was soon revealed that the man had serious knee injuries. The ambulance rushed Gerry McCafferty to the Victoria Hospital, where he received emergency treatment for a broken nose, and arm. In addition, both his knees had had holes drilled in them. Gerry would never be a runner again and it would be a very long time before, if ever, he would even walk again.

At the same time as he was in surgery, two happy lads in Livingston were drinking a toast to Frank Muir. They had done a good job and looked forward to receiving the balance of the agreed money from him.

The police in Kirkcaldy did all the usual checking around the doors, but no one had seen or heard anything. Surprise, surprise, the public knew a serious attack would probably be gang related and possibly it would be a drug gang that was involved in some dodgy dealing, the local residents were nervous about talking to the police.

They had tried to contact Mary McCaferty, Gerry's sister, but they did not get an answer; so they then called Billy Booth, whom they knew was one of Gerry's friends. Billy received the call on his cell phone.

The police, explained to him about Gerry's 'accident' and that holes had been bored into both his knees.

"Who the fuck did that," he said, but the police just told him that they were still looking into the case. Billy ran home as fast as he could to tell Mary, who was shocked at his news.

"Why and who," she shouted out, and he told her that the cops told him that they were looking into it.

"Why didn't the police call me?" she said, Billy told her they had, but got no answer.

"Shit, I had forgotten to take my phone with me when I went out to the shop to get milk," was her reply.

Mary's, eyes were full of tears, as she rushed to the Victoria hospital to be at Gerry's bedside. He was still in surgery when she got there, and she had to wait a couple of hours before seeing him. When she did get into the ward he was in, she said, "Who could have done this to you Gerry?" However, Gerry was saying nothing. He was thinking that it was either Frank, or one of his buyers, who had found out he had been cutting in on the supply.

There was going to be a long wait before he would try to get his own back on the bastard, whoever it was. Gerry, thought to himself, one day, I will find out, and get my revenge. No one fucks with a McCaferty and gets away with it.

Mary continued to try to question him without any luck. Gerry told Mary that he was very sore and tired and that she should go home, and come back later when he felt better. She was still none the wiser as to how or why he had been attacked so badly.

The police thought that possibly a drug gang had attacked Gerry after they had found out they had been cheated by him. It was obviously not a normal mugging, as both his knees had holes drilled in them. Typical major drug fallout they thought, but they could not link him with a gang.

Gerry himself was not saying anything to them, other than that; he did not see whom it was that attacked him. All he told them was that he had been driven away in a van somewhere, he did not know where. When the attack had happened, he had fallen unconscious. He said he was then obviously returned to the place he was found by the police officer, and the next thing he remembered was wakening up in hospital.

The police eventually put it down as just another local drug deal gone wrong, and cold filed the case away. Some thought that maybe Gerry had received what he deserved, or it could even have been a very angry parent, that found out about his dealing. They hoped that something would come up in the next few months or so.

Very soon after Gerry's 'accident', Frank Muir disappeared after he had been abducted outside his favourite pub. The police had no idea as to why or what had happened to him. Frank Muir would not be heard of, or seen again. That is, until a skeleton is uncovered on a moor in the north west of Scotland, some five years later.

Gerry was not happy at Mary staying with him; he told her that if Frank was to come after him, she might be in danger. He told her that she should move well away from the area.

Mary began searching for a new job and eventually found a suitable one in Dingwall, in the north of

Scotland.

Because of Mary's qualifications, the pay offered was good, so she would be able to rent a flat up there. She applied and was told that she had the job if she could start right away.

Mary said, "as soon as I find a place to stay I can get there."

CHAPTER 26

North Scotland, 2019.

It is March and gamekeepers, along with workers from Forestry Commission Scotland, are burning heather on the Barrylairg Estate, in the North West of Scotland. This controlled burning is carried out to protect the environment on the moors and hillsides of the Highlands.

Suddenly, a cry is heard from one of the fire control beaters, "over here!"

The fire chief is summoned, along with the Estate manager, Craig Browne.
Twenty meters from a rough track, they find out what the beater was shouting about, the remains of a human skeleton.

Detective Inspector Ian Ewing attends the find up on the moors.
After a couple of days, DI Ewing and his team are still trying to investigate who the body could possibly be, when a call comes through from foren-

sics.

Their investigation revealed that it was a male, aged approximately late thirties, early forties, and the result of his death was a bullet through the side of his head. They also said that they think that the body was possibly dumped there in the region of five years ago. In addition, that they had found a ring on the remains. They thought, as it had initials on it, it might help to identify the victim.

Immediately, DI Ewing sends a squad car over to collect the ring, and after inspection, it revealed the initials FM, had been engraved on it.

On checking through files, from five years previously, they found out that, in twenty fourteen, a couple of men had mysteriously disappeared in the central belt of Scotland. However, the name of one of the men was Frank Muir, from Kirkcaldy, Fife. The same initials as the ring. DI Ewing now had a name to tie in with the ring found on the skeleton, and believed that it might be him.

DI Ian wanted to find out more about Frank Muir, so he checked with Kirkcaldy police and they informed him about a Gerry McCaferty, who had been seriously injured and that Frank Muir, before he disappeared, had been a suspect in the assault,. They also told him that Gerry's sister now lived in Dingwall and that she had been a lover of Frank. They passed on Mary's address to DI Ewing who then decided to interview Mary McCaferty.

As he knew that they had been lovers, did she

know if he was still alive?

After the short drive over to Dingwall, a small town at the south end of the Cromarty Firth, with a population of five and a half thousand.

DI Ian parked in the car lot allotted to the apartment blocks. Mary stayed in apartment 4d, on the fourth floor of a modern block, in Church Lane. He was glad there was a lift. Mary answered the door and after he introduced himself, she invited him inside.

DI Ian was surprised at how good-looking Mary was; she had long beautiful red hair and a nice body. He thought, I may be sixty but it does not mean that I cannot admire a nice looking woman.

The conversation began with DI Ewing explaining why he was there, and then asked her if she could explain about her relationship with Frank.

Mary said, she had met Frank on one of his visits to Billy's flat, where she was staying, and they had hit it off right away.

"So why didn't you move in with him?" The DI asked.

"Billy had let me stay with him and did not charge rent, other than keeping him happy. Frank told me that he did not want anyone living in his flat, as it would interfere with his business. He thought that I did not know what he did for a living, in fact all his friends knew."

Without giving out too much information, DI Ian said to her that they were still waiting on confirmation of the identification of the skeleton, so he would let her know when they had it.

"It would certainly put my mind to rest as I have always wondered what had happened to him," she said,

After about another half an hour of questions and not many forthcoming answers, other than that she was working in a local hairdresser shop now, she said, "it is next door to the Royal bank of Scotland, in the High Street. Since Billy, I have not had a steady boyfriend.

She did ask DI Ian jokingly "are you single?" He replied that he was, but he was a bit too old for her, "Maybe if I had been twenty years younger," he said.

She replied that she preferred older men anyway, and they both had a good laugh. DI Ian realised that on this visit, Mary was going to be of no more help to him concerning his case, so he said to her that he had to go before he changed his mind, and they laughed again, they said their goodbyes and DI Ian Ewing left with a big grin on his face and thinking, if only.

He then heads back to Inverness.
Through DNA evidence, it was soon revealed that the skeleton was that of a John Williams,

After checking with the Home Office, it was revealed that a John Williams, 'alias Frank Muir' and an Alan Deans had flown to Spain in Twenty Fourteen.

It confirmed Ian's thoughts that Frank Muir was

more than likely still alive and probably living a new life in Spain.

DI Ewing is now thinking that they had been responsible for the murder of John Williams.

CHAPTER 27

DI Ian Ewing thinks that a trip to Spain would help clear things up.

After consulting with his superiors, DI Ewing had received permission to go to Spain to check on Frank Muir and Alan Deans. He booked flights and then hotel accommodation in the town of Mojacher.

While there, he discovered that Frank had taken on the name of John Williams and he had opened a bar called Paradise. In addition, Alan Deans was his manager.

With the information he gathered there, he knew that the Scottish Police would have to go through the Home office in the UK, and this system could not guarantee that the Spanish Guardia would arrest Frank and Alan with the murder of John Williams.

On his return to Scotland, he suggested to CI Burns that he could go to see Mary McCaferty again and let her know that Frank Muir was still alive and living in Spain.

CI Burns told him, "good idea pal," and laughed as he continued, "After you told me how beautiful she is, behave yourself."

Ian called Mary. As she answered her phone she said, "Hi this is Mary." Ian told her it was DI Ian Ewing calling and that he had some information she may like to hear.
He said.
"Can I call on you later tomorrow?" Mary told him that would be fine and that as it is Saturday; she is only working the morning shift.
"Can you say anything now?" she asked,
"No sorry, not over the phone, since you are free in the afternoon I can be there anytime after twelve-thirty." Mary told him that one o'clock would suit her perfectly, both of them agreed.
DI Ian said, "See you then," and with a wee smirk on his face, he ended the call. Maybe I could invite her for lunch he thought, and then said, behave yourself Ian, you are old enough to be her dad.

Saturday was a day off for Ian, and he used it to catch up and do some housework before going out shopping. He needed to get his cupboard and fridge supplies topped up again after his trip to Spain. He had it all finished by twelve o'clock and wondered if he should have his lunch before he goes to Dingwall. No, I will wait and see how it goes when I get there, he decided.

As it was only a twenty-five minute drive to Ding-wall, he had time to go and top up his petrol tank.

He had left it only a quarter full when he went away on holiday, maybe I should put it through the car wash as well, he thought.

Almost dead on one o'clock, he was knocking on Mary's front door, and she answered almost immediately, she told DI Ian that he was very prompt. "Must be the policeman in you," she said, "come on in."

As Ian followed her, he noticed the nice legs under a short skirt. She sat down in an armchair and beckoned DI Ian to sit opposite her on the settee, "so what news have you got for me Inspector?"

He replied by saying, "please call me Ian," Mary nodded and smiled at him.

With a perfect view, of her long legs, a slightly flushed, Ian continued to tell her all about Frank Muir, who was now calling himself John Williams. In addition, that he owned his own Café bar in Mojacar, Spain, and an Alan Deans was the manager. He went on to say to her that Alan was one of the men who had attacked her brother Gerry. "Wow," said Mary, "and you say that they are in a town called Mojacar."

She went on to ask a few more questions about the two, and appeared to be interested in Ian's replies. Mary then asked Ian if he would like a cup of tea and a biscuit, so Ian took a chance and said that he was a wee bit hungry, would she like to have lunch with him instead.

She replied that she would love to have lunch

with him, "much better than eating on your own, isn't it Ian?"

He asked her if she knew a nice restaurant that they could go too. Mary told him that there was a wonderful little place, but it was about five miles out of town. Ian thinking that it may be better going to a quiet place where Mary would not be questioned about the older man she was with, told her that it would be no problem.

On the drive to the restaurant, Ian had an occasional glance at those legs; there was a bit more showing while she was in the car. Mary knew she was showing her legs, and she knew that Ian was obviously having a wee peek and liking what he saw.

When they reached the restaurant, just before two pm, Ian walked round and opened her door, yes she is thinking; older men are so much nicer and polite.

They walked inside and Ian asked for a table in a quite corner. There was a strange look from the server, as she showed them to a table near to a window. Ian stood behind Mary and helped her with the chair by sliding it gentle in as she sat down. Bloody hell, she is thinking, I could marry this one.

Ian asked her what kind of wine she liked and she said Rosé was her favourite.

A server came over with the menus and asked if they would like something to drink, Ian ordered the Mateus, and asked her to give them a few minutes to decide what they want to eat.

Mary is again thinking that this man is good; he even knows a nice Rosé wine. They both went for the steak Diane and after the order was taken, Mary said that she would go fifty-fifty on the bill. "Absolutely no way," Ian told her. He would not have asked her out if he knew she was going to do that. "Taking a lady out to lunch is something I have not done for a very long time, and I am enjoying every minute."

After they finished eating, they sat chatting a little while. As Ian just wanted to spend more time with her, he suggested that they go for a walk. Mary agreed and told him there was a nice walkway alongside the River Peffery in Dingwall; she would show him where it was. As she was getting in his car, she had opened her legs a little and he noticed a flash of her white panties as he gently closed the door.

By the time they reached the walkway, it was now a quarter to four and a little chilly; Mary slipped her arm onto his as they walked along the narrow path. She began asking more questions about his trip to Spain, and Ian told her all about his time in Mojacar, and how beautiful it was.

After the drive back, when they reached Mary's apartment, she said to Ian to come in for a coffee before going home, but he said that it was not necessary. She laughed and said.

"It was an order Ian, not a request."

As they entered the front door, Mary went into the kitchen to put the coffee on. When she came back out, she said to Ian, to keep an eye on it for her, I have to go to the bathroom. Ian told her he would, no problem. A few minutes later, she came back into the lounge wearing something he could only describe as a very short dressing gown, which was tied loosely, in a bow round her waist. She drifted past him into the kitchen. The sight of her in a lack of clothes, and her scent, sent Ian's mind buzzing. He took his jacket off and loosened his tie, then sat down on the couch again.

Mary brought the two coffees through and sat on the chair opposite Ian, as she did this she folded her legs up onto it. Ian noticed that the white panties were no longer visible.

They talked a bit until she finished her coffee, and then she stood up, as she went over to where Ian was sitting, she untied the bow on her dressing gown letting it fall open revealing her beautiful naked body. Then Mary kneeled on the couch alongside him and gave him a very sensual kiss, and ran her tongue over his lips, as she did this she put a leg over Ian's legs and sat astride on his lap. As she kissed him, she began moving her body back and fro. He is now thinking that he has died and gone to heaven, however, the erection he was getting brought him back down to earth.

Ian Ewing was about to have his first sex since the loss of his wife some twenty years previous.

Sunday mid morning, Inverness, finds Ian sitting in his favourite armchair nursing a cup of tea in his hands, he is thinking over his actions from last night and wondering if he had done the right thing.

His phone beeps and he notices the messenger app from Mary, he tapped the little picture and read the message.

Good morning, my darling Ian, I hope you had a wonderful evening, I certainly did. Please do not feel guilty my dear, after all it was me who came on to you, and I am so happy I did. I can only tell you that it was the best day I have ever spent with a man, so thank you. I realise that you were a bit concerned last night, so I am giving you time to think it over.

On Wednesday, I am going to leave and spend the next two or three weeks with my Aunt in Ireland. I will get in touch when I come home. Please do not answer this text. Bye, xxx

Bloody hell, thought Ian, what have I got myself into, good job I do not have to answer right away, I am not sure what to say.

CHAPTER 28

Mary's quest.

Early Wednesday morning saw Mary McCaferty drive to Inverness bus station, where she would leave her car in a parking lot. Then take a bus heading to Glasgow, Buchanan Street, bus depot. From there she would get a taxi to the airport. However, she would not be boarding a plane for Dublin, Ireland; her ticket said Almeria, Spain,

She had taken in all Ian had said, and had booked her flight as soon as possible. She wanted to see Frank and his pal Alan, before the Spanish police had the chance to arrest them.

The clothes she had with her were all thin summer stuff so she managed to get them all in her carry on case along with a blond wig. As she would not have to wait for a booked in case at Almeria, this would help her get to the car rental before most other passengers. The flight left Glasgow on time and arrived in Almeria ten minutes early.

Once in her hire car, she programmed the hotel into the car sat nav, and as she had also studied the directions beforehand, she immediately heads north to Mojacar.

Mary had been to Spain a few times and had driven there before, so she had experience about driving on the right side of the road. The sat nav told her every turn and directed her right to the Hotel El Puntazo II, the same place where Ian had said he had stayed.

Between getting through the airport quickly, and the drive to Mojacar, she had probably knocked about twenty minutes of the time it had taken DI Ewing.

As she got into her bed that evening, she was thinking about Ian and their day together, Ian was a true gentleman. If he only knew what she had in her mind now, however, there was no way in the world she could have told him.

Thursday morning and Mary was up bright and early, she had her plan to attend to, and was desperate to get on with it. After breakfast, she went back to her room, only to emerge thirty minute later with the most wonderful head of blond hair. Being an accomplished hairdresser, she had bought the best she could; it was made from real human hair, and that was a major part of her plan.

She remembered that DI Ewing had told her that Alan was on days and Frank nights, that was to be a big help for what she intended.

About eleven-thirty a beautiful longhaired blond

woman walked into the Paradise Bar, Alan's head turned immediately and he did not hesitate to escort her to a table.

"Hi I'm Alan, can I get something for you this morning,"

She said that she would like a café con leche thank you. Alan scurried off to get her coffee, he is thinking to himself, wow, I would not mind getting into her pants. This was just what Mary had intended him to think.

He soon returned with the coffee, and started chatting to Mary, who had introduced herself as 'Megan Murphy.' She even had those initials embroidered on a silk necktie she had on, nice wee touch thought Alan.

He had been hooked right in, thought Mary, alias 'Megan', as she gave him her best smile, now to throw the net over him.

She said, "This is my first time on holiday, since I divorced my husband, and I do not know my way about here, maybe if I need help finding my way around you could give me advice."

Alan is now thinking that he has landed a good one this time, not realizing that it was in fact the other way about. He said to her that he would be delighted to help by taking her out for dinner, but it would have to be later in the day as he worked the day shift here.

"I am the manager here, but when it is not the tourist season, with less staff, we have to do more," She replied. "Oh that is all right Alan, as long as your wife does not mind."

Things get better and better thought Alan, as he told her he was single and unattached.

'Megan' knew this but she was manipulating him into a sense of confidence in her.

As she had another coffee, she said to Alan,

"I heard that the steak here was very good, so for lunch today, I think I will have one, medium rare." "Certainly 'Megan'," said Alan, "I will go get it my-self when you are ready, just let me know."

She waited for about half an hour, and then said that she was ready to eat. Alan went off to get her lunch, and when he returned with the steak, 'Megan' accidently knocked the knife of the plate, "Oops sorry," she said.

Alan picked it up and said that he would fetch a clean one for her. "Perfect, thank you Alan."

When he returned with the clean steak knife, he said to her that he would have to go back into the kitchen for a little while. However, before he left, she said to him that she would look forward to see-ing him tonight. "I can meet you outside the Irish restaurant at six-thirty Alan."

As soon as he turned to go, she placed the still clean knife, carefully in her handbag and she re-moved another similar one to eat her steak.

When she had finished eating, she went to pay Carol at her cash desk, and made a point of calling on Alan. When he came out, she gave him a big kiss on the cheek and walked out, saying, see you later Alan. Which was noticed by Carol who said, "well you are certainly a fast worker Alan, you lucky bugger."

When Frank, alias 'John,' arrived later that day for his evening shift, Alan could hardly wait to tell him about a stunning blond that came in earlier, and that he had a date with her tonight.

"I think she was impressed that I was the manager here," he said.

'John' said, "Fuck, if she had come in at night I could have told her I owned the place and made that date with her, you lucky bastard."

Alan just laughed and told him, "Tough luck pal." Unknown to both men, it was part of Mary's plan to get them jealous of each other.

Alan arrived first, just two minutes before 'Megan,' he suggested that since they were already at the Irish place, they should eat there as well, and 'Megan' agreed.

The date went well, and after they had a bottle of wine, Alan said that they could go for a little walk along the front. This they did and during the stroll, Alan asked her if she would like to have a coffee at his place. 'Megan' said that he was taking things a little fast and to leave it for a few days, Alan smiled to her and said "Okay."

He is thinking if it was only going to take a couple of days, he could wait to get this beauty into his bed.

As they walked back, Alan suggested that they pop into the Paradise, to which 'Megan' says,

"No thanks Alan, I am still tired after the traveling. You should go in and I will get a taxi to my hotel." Bugger thought Alan; he wanted to show her off to 'John.'

She gave him a wee kiss and said to him that she would see him tomorrow. Alan then went into the Paradise to do his bragging, and told 'John' that he would have her in his bed within a couple of days.

"Fuck you," said 'John.'

Mary was smiling as she travelled back to the hotel; all I have to do is too keep clear of Frank for a few days then put the next phase of my plan into action.

Back in her room, she took the knife out of her bag and wrapped it in a tissue, it was important to her plan.

Lunchtime Friday saw her in the Paradise again, with Alan fussing over Megan. Carol is thinking how stupid he looks; she has him running after her. Alan asked her if she wanted to go out with him that evening, but 'Megan' told him she had a little headache so could they leave it another day. Reluctantly, Alan agreed, "Maybe see you tomorrow."

'Megan' had lunch, and then made a fuss of kissing Alan as she was leaving, and saying, see you tomorrow. Carol is behind her desk shaking her head and thinking, she has you on a string Alan.

Next day while she is at the Paradise, 'Megan', arranges to meet Alan that night, again at the same place. That way Mary knew she would be staying clear of Frank again

The two meet that Saturday evening, this time she asked Alan what his place looked like. Perfect opportunity thinks Alan; he says to her,

"After dinner, why don't you come and see for yourself."

Later they walk to Alan's apartment, and soon after they are inside, he brings out a bottle of wine and asks her if she would like a glass. She told him that she preferred Rosé, but that she would still have a glass of the white. By the time the bottle is empty, 'Megan' has slid closer to Alan and he starts to fondle her breasts, it is not long before they are both in his bed having sex.

Later he offers to walk her to her hotel but she says that it is okay, "see you tomorrow Alan."

For most of the Sunday morning, Mary is lying at the poolside of her hotel. She has lunch there, and by mid afternoon, she is walking into the Paradise. Carol says, "hi Megan," and shows her to a table. She tells her that Alan has an ear-to-ear smile on his face today.

'Megan' smiled and asked for a café con leche

Alan appeared next and sat down beside her, "Thank you for a wonderful evening 'Megan'."

She said to him that she had enjoyed it as well, "maybe tomorrow night, I could come back to your place again."

"Aye sure," he said, "but what's wrong with to-night."

She replied that she was attending a ladies evening at her hotel, but she would love to see him tomorrow. 'Megan' told him that she would finish her **café con leche** and then she had to go get prepared for her evening. Alan suggested she come to his apartment about seven to seven thirty tomorrow, and this was agreed. After she finished her coffee she got up, paid Carol and gave Alan another smacker on his lips, "see you tomorrow night hunny," she said.

Mary's plan is coming along nicely; by Alan missing getting her into his bed tonight, she is getting him a bit frustrated,

Mary enjoys the rest of the afternoon by the pool, and contemplates the next few days before heading home, she is happy with her plans meantime.

Monday evening could not come quick enough for Alan; he is desperate to see his 'Megan' again. Of course, getting her into his bed is a big plus for him.

He hears a knock at the door, and almost falls over his own feet, hurrying to open it. 'Megan' is standing there in a very short mini dress and a low cut blouse, showing a fair bit of her ample breasts.

"Wow, you look fantastic 'Megan,' come in, come in." She thanks him and enters the apartment.
By the time they had finished off the bottle of Rosé wine, he was sitting close to her and fondling her breasts, they were soon back in Alan's bed again, this time though she stayed all night.

Next morning he was up early and was in the

middle of making breakfast, when 'Megan' walked into the kitchen, completely naked. Fucking hell, he thinks what a beauty, and how lucky am I to have slept with her all night. 'Megan' smiled and said to him that she was going for a quick shower before breakfast. Alan told her to hurry, as it was nearly ready.

'Megan' had on his dressing gown when she came back from her shower, and sat down to a bacon and egg breakfast made by Alan. As soon as he finished his, he told her that he had to go, as it was time to open up the bar. He says, "However, You can stay here as long as you wish Megan."

She thanked him and said that she would get dressed in a wee while and head back to her hotel to change her clothes.

"I will pop in for lunch, so see you then," she said.

Alan told her he would look forward to it.

Before she left the apartment, Mary pulled out a couple of strands of blond hair from her wig; she placed one under a pillow on the bed and another in a comb in the bathroom cabinet.

It is now Tuesday, so time to step up the action she thinks. After a change of clothes at the hotel, she headed back to the Paradise Café bar. There is an even bigger smile on Alan's face now; she did not think that was possible. She ordered a tostada and cafe con leche and sat at a table in full view of Carol's desk, where Mary would make sure Carol had a good view.

Alan was soon over to see her and as he sat down,

she told him that their relationship had to end.

"What" he shouted "Why?"

She lied when she told him that she had been seeing another man that had taken her fancy, and that was where she had been the other night, not at women's meeting in the hotel. "Last night was my way of saying thank you Alan, but sorry, we are finished. Anyway, I am sure you enjoyed yourself, didn't you?"

"You mean you were having me on, when you told me that you had enjoyed our sex last night."

"I did enjoy it Alan, but not as much as with him, he is terrific in bed."

Alan is now fuming and shouting at her,

"Get out of my bar you fucking bitch."

All this was to Mary's benefit, and right where she knew Carol would see, and hear it all.

Mary walked out without finishing her tostada, but her smile was even bigger than the one Alan had on earlier. Carol is just standing behind her cash desk, mouth wide open and her chin almost touching her chest. Alan walks straight past her and into the kitchen, slamming the door behind him.

"Fuck me," Carol is saying aloud, "what just happened there."

The people at the other three tables that were occupied, just smiled, and started whispering to each other.

Meanwhile Mary is heading back to her hotel to prepare herself for going to see this special man in the evening. When 'John' arrived in for his shift, Carol went straight over to him to let him know what had happened earlier. She said that Alan was in a very bad mood, so please do not wind him up. 'John' said that he would tread carefully with him but was smiling when he said it.

When 'John" went into the kitchen Alan did not say a word, he just stomped past him slamming the kitchen door again, and out the front of the restaurant.

A strange thing happened later that evening when 'John' was working; this beautiful blond woman came into the Paradise; she walked straight up to him and said, "Hello Frank".

Now it was his turn to have his chin drop.

"What the fuck! Is that you Mary, what are you doing here?"

He quickly ushered her to a table in the corner, away from other patrons in the bar, and said,

"I hardly recognised you with your hair gone blond, you look great. What are you doing here?" He then went on to explain that his name was now 'John Williams,' and she should use that name from now on. "That's funny," said Mary,"I have changed mine to 'Megan'."

The penny now dropped and 'John' said,

"You mean you are the one that dumped Alan earlier on today."

She said that she was that same person, and that she only did it after she realised that he, Frank, was here. Another wee lie by Mary. Frank said,

"Carol told me everything that was said between you two and that you had told Alan that you had found someone much better in bed than he was. Is that true Mary, oops sorry, 'Megan'?"

She told him that it was true, and started laughing.

"Christ Megan, you really pissed Alan off earlier, Carol told me he was going mad and that he would kill the other man if he could find him. Mind you, we did have some great sex in those days."

As she knew that it would be very late before he finished work, she suggested that they meet up the next afternoon, she did not mention the fact that she was due to fly home the next evening.

Frank told her to remember to call him 'John' and that he would be delighted, and should he come to her hotel? She answered by saying that she would like to see his home, so could she go there?

He was very happy to oblige, he told her how to find his home, and they arranged for her too arrive at one pm. This would suit him, as he would not get home from work until two or three in the morning.

Just as Mary was about to leave, Carol had come back for her phone that she had forgotten. She noticed 'John' was with 'Megan' and asked her what was going on, and then it struck her,

"Don't tell me that this is the man, you told Alan was better at sex than him."

'Megan' said, "So what," and told her he was that man, "and yes, he is so much better in bed than

Alan is."

Carol said, "Fuck you Megan," then grabbed her phone and walked out saying, "wait until I tell Alan tomorrow."

Megan said, "Oh dear, sorry Fra, sorry John, have I just dropped you in it?"

He told her that after seeing her in the afternoon, he would have a chat with Alan at night when he gets into work. I will tell him that we used to be lovers and you were lying about being with me the other night, because you were hoping to get together with me again. I will tell him I am not interested. He went on to say,

"Maybe you had best stay clear of the Paradise for a while 'Megan', let's not wind him up too much."

To which she replied that she would stay well clear, and luckily, she had not told him which hotel she was staying at.

All the time Mary is thinking to herself that Scotland should be far enough away.

She lied once more. "It is an amazing coincidence that I found you here Frank, especially after me going out with Alan."

He tells her it was a bigger surprise to him, but that he was happy to see her again.

"But please stop calling me Frank, its 'John'."

They chat for a few more minutes then Diane, a server, calls over to him that he is required in the kitchen. They say their goodbyes and share a kiss, "see you tomorrow Fra' oops sorry, 'John'."

He smiles and tells her he will look forward to it.

Mary's next step was to get back to her hotel and pack most of her clothes into her carry-on case, ready for the flight home the next day. After seeing Frank, alias 'John', she would have to make a quick getaway.

CHAPTER 29

Mary's last day in Spain.

Wednesday morning at breakfast, Mary is thinking about how well her plan is going, and she is looking forward to bedding Frank Muir once more.

As she has to be out of her room by eleven am, she carries her case out to the car and puts it in the boot to keep it out of sight. She then walks down the road in the other direction from the Paradise, to find the tapas bar that Ian Ewing had told her about. Mary took her time over a couple of their wonderful tapas and two café con leche's.

At twelve thirty, she pays her bar tab, walked back to her car and then drives towards Franks home, and parked further down the street, and half way between there and the bar.

She made sure that 'John's' neighbours who were sitting on their balcony, noticed her as she walked up to his door. Frank answered the knock and opened it to a beautiful Mary McCaferty standing there in the same clothes she had been wearing when she was at Alan's home. She got the same reaction from 'John' as she did from Alan.

"Wow, you look fantastic 'Megan', welcome to my home."

"Thank you 'John' lovely to see you again," she said aloud, as she entered the apartment.

He had remembering her taste in wine went over to the table and opened the bottle of Mateus Rosé.

"So you remembered Frank," she said.

"How could I forget Mary, we shared many a bottle of Rosé." In private they have went back to calling each other by their right names.

They had only drunk one glass each before she knelt before Frank, who was sitting on the couch next to her, and undid his zipper. She had done this a few times in the past, and Frank was looking forward to what he knew, she was about to do to him. Very soon, they entered his bedroom to continue with their sex.

By the time it was over Frank was exhausted and lay back well satisfied. Mary said that she had a big surprise for him, but she had to go to the bathroom first. She grabbed her bag on the way.

When she came out of the bathroom, she had removed the blond wig, and now had a pair of gloves on her hands. Frank was admiring the almost naked body of this beautiful red haired woman, when she said to him, "Frankie, lie back and close your eyes tight for the special surprise I have for you,"

He was wondering what kind of surprise it could be with her wearing those gloves, but he smiled and did as she had told him.

With his eyes closed tight, she pulled the covers slowly off him, and this was when Mary said,
"I am going to enjoy this Frank, this is for Gerry."
Then she thrust the knife deep into his heart. Franks eyes burst wide open and stared at her in disbelief, as he gasped his last breath, he heard her say,

"That will teach you to fuck with the McCaferty family Frankie."

Frank Muir really is dead this time, she said to herself,

She pulled another couple of strands from the blond wig and laid one right between his legs, next to his now slumped penis. She also left one on the pillow next to him and the last one behind his left ear. Her next moves were to very carefully remove her gloves, and put on the shower cap she had brought with her. She then went and had a quick shower to wash all Frank's blood from her naked body. When that was done, she quickly dressed, made sure that she had put the gloves and shower cap back in her bag, put the blond wig back on and headed out the door shouting back, for the benefit of his neighbours.

"See you tomorrow John, thanks for a lovely time."

The blonde-haired 'Megan' walked back down the street got into her car and drove round the corner to be closer to the Paradise Café Bar.

As she walked in Carol shouted to her, "you've got a hard neck 'Megan', Alan told you to fuck off, I have not had the chance to tell him it was John that you were with, so go before he finds out."

'Megan' called back and told her she wished to apologise to Alan.

Just then, he came out of the kitchen and before he could say anything, 'Megan' walked over to him, and as she placed a gloved hand on his shoulder, said that she wanted to say that she was very sorry,

"Could you take me back, because 'John' wasn't that good."

Alan was taken aback a little bit, by what he had just heard,

"You mean that it was 'John' you were fucking with."

She said as she rubbed his shoulder,

"Yes it was Alan, and I am sorry."

He said, "Fuck off Megan, you are just a whore, we are finished." as he pushed past her, he said,

"I am going to kill that fucking bastard, 'John'."

Carol went running after him, but Alan told her to get back into the bar, as she did this, she passed 'Megan' who was on her way out. She told her never to show her face in the bar again,

"Alan is right 'Megan', you are just a fucking whore, just piss off."

Mary went straight to her car, started it up and steered it out of Mojacar, in the direction of Almeria airport.

At the same time as she was doing this Alan is thumping his fists on 'John's' door and shouting,

"come out you bastard, I'm going to kill you."
Just then he tries the door, it opens up and he rushes inside, which is noticed by the neighbours. A few seconds later a shout is heard, then a moment of silence.

Inside the house, Alan had seen that 'John' was not in his sitting room, so he must be in his bed yet. He walks straight into the bedroom and sees 'John' on his bed with a knife in his chest and blood all over the sheets. His immediate reaction was to shout aloud. "Ahhh."

A couple of neighbours rush in and they see Alan standing over the body.

As they grab Alan, he is shouting that he did not do it. Nevertheless, they keep a hold of him and call the Guardia. When they arrive, the neighbours inform them what they had heard and found when they got in; Alan is arrested for the murder of 'John Williams,' all the time screaming his innocence.
"It must have been that blond bitch," he is shouting.

However one of the neighbours told the Guardia that she had seen a woman walk out of the house about five or ten minutes earlier, and shout back inside, see you tomorrow 'John', thanks for a lovely time, so he must have been alive then."

Alan was bundled, not too carefully, into the police car, still claiming his innocence. Later it would be Alan's fingerprints on the handle of the weapon used, and in fact, that knife was one that belonged to the Paradise Café Bar, where Alan had left shouting that he was going to kill 'John'.

As well as Carol, there were customers at the bar who had witnessed the scene and were all prepared to swear this in court. No matter how much Alan pleaded his innocence, he was well and truly screwed. Later they had even found some of 'John's' blood on the shoulder of his T-shirt, and he could not explain how it got there. It looked like he would be in Spanish prison for a very long time.

'Megan' has disappeared.

That evening, as Mary boarded a flight for Glasgow, she did not realise just how well her plan had worked. She thought that maybe she would have to wait for a week or two to find out, however she would know much sooner than that.

Now for the final part of my plan she said to herself, As soon as she landed at Glasgow, she sent a text to Ian Ewing saying that, her aunt had booked a holiday to Greece. So she had had to come back to Glasgow quicker than she thought she would have done.

Mary took a taxi to the Holiday Inn Express, Sauchiehall Street, and stayed there overnight. As it was close to the bus depot, she would be ready for an early trip back to Inverness, on Thursday morning. On arriving there, she would pick up her own car to drive home to Dingwall.

CHAPTER 30

Ian learns of the murder.

It was late in the evening that DI Ian read the text from Mary and realised that he would have to make up his mind about her very soon. However, what to say and do was his problem now, I will not answer the text yet, he says to himself.

As he continues with his work, Mary McCaferty keeps popping up in his mind; he is thinking that there is something about her that he cannot work out. Later that afternoon, a text came in to DI Ewing's office from The Home Office; it stated that, Frank Muir, the man that they had been enquiring about had been murdered in his bed.

His restaurant manager, an Alan Deans, had stabbed him to death. It also stated, just before the murder, a blonde female had been spotted in the proximity, but that person had disappeared. However, the Guardia had arrested the bar manager

Alan Deans, as he was caught in the bedroom of the victim.

Local witnesses had heard him say that he was going to kill his boss. In addition, one of the servers at the bar had heard him say the same as he left to go after Mr. Williams.

DI Ewing talked to his CI and said, "There was no sign of any blond woman when I was there sir, so she must have just come on to the scene after I left."

Alec suggested that they both go over every thing again and see if they can come up with a way of finding this woman.

DI Ian was back in his office reading his copy of the report, and wondering how they, in Scotland, had any chance of finding this blond woman.

Just then he was startled with a ping on his phone, It was Mary McCaferty. I cannot handle that just now, he thinks, so he texted her back and said that he was in the middle of a very important enquiry, and that he would be busy all day.

Now, inside his head, Ian's mind pinged,
"Bloody Mary McCaferty," he says aloud.
"What was that Ian," said Alec Burns who had just walked into the office.
"Oh, it is only a wee thought that struck me sir."
"Out with it Ian, if you have something on your mind I want to know."
Ian goes on to explain some of the details of the day he had spent with Mary, carefully leaving out

what had happened in her apartment that night. He went on to say that he had not realised it at the time, but she had been asking many questions about Frank Muir.

"Do you think that she could be connected Ian,"

"I do not know sir, but something is not quite right."

After Alec leaves, Ian gets pen and paper at the ready for his notes.

Firstly, where should I start, do I contact Mary? No, best not to, if she is involved in this murder in any way, I do not want her to suspect I know anything until we have concrete evidence.

Now where should I begin to find out, he is asking himself again. Next question, did Mary really go to Ireland, or did she end up flying to Spain? Yes, it is possible.

Could she be the blond haired woman who had caused the rift between Alan Deans and Frank Muir? Yes, that is possible.

Could she have actually murdered Frank, and blamed it on Alan? Yes also possible, but the evidence says not likely.

Did Mary have enough time to get to Spain and back to Scotland? Definitely yes, then it had dawned on Ian that the Almeria flights from Glasgow, are on Wednesdays. The same day that she said she was going to Ireland, and the same day she came back.

Ian then sent a short text to Mary, saying that he

was still very busy but he promised to be in touch soon. He is hoping that she will accept his excuse for not meeting with her. Mary hears the ping from her phone, but as she is in the middle of a customer's hair appointment, she has to wait a few minutes before reading it.

Her reaction is exactly as DI Ian had hoped it would be, she was just so pleased to have heard from him. The rest of her day, she would have a big smile on her face, not realizing what was on Ian's mind at this time.

Guardia Civil report.

Chief Inspector Burns was waiting on the report from the UK Authorities when Ian walked into his office, after knocking on his door.

The Home Office had given him the exact information that he had expected. Mary McCaferty had flown from Glasgow to Spain and returned back one week later.

The UK Authorities had translated a full report from the Guardia Civil in Spain, and it stated that the weapon used to kill John Williams, had been a steak knife, which had come from the Paradise Café Bar. As far as they were concerned, they had the murderer in custody.

(End of Report).

The two officers just looked at each other, and then Alec said, "This Mary McCaferty is one devious woman Ian. What she has done, or had encouraged to be done is still a mystery."

Alec told Ian that he should now arrange for Mary to come in for questioning,

"We need to find out what she has been up to, so do you want to interrogate her or shall I?" he asked.

Ian breathed a sigh of relief and said to Alec,

"It would be best if you did it, as I have already met with her. A more senior officer would possibly frighten her a little. I will wait and watch from behind the two way mirror."

Just as Mary McCaferty was about to leave for her lunch hour, a police car arrived at the hairdressers shop where she worked. The officer asked her to accompany him to the police station at Burnett Road, Inverness, to assist them in their inquiries. She is taken by surprise at the request, and asks why?

She was told that it was just to help them in their inquiries, and Chief Inspector Alec Burns would explain to her what they required. Mary is wondering why it was not her lovely man Ian that would be there. However, she says nothing other than, "I hope you will bring me back to Dingwall."

The police told her that a car would return her when they were finished.

They arrive at Burnett Road about half an hour later and she was escorted in to a waiting room.

Ten minutes later, she is directed into the interrogation room to where CI Burns was waiting at a desk. He notices how stunning this red head is.

He stood up and politely said to Mary,

"Please take a seat Ms McCaferty,"

As she sits down, Mary is asking what this is all about.

CI Burns tells her that it is to do with a murder in Mojacar, Spain, and he was about to ask her questions on the case.

He went on to say that the conversation was going to be recorded. The machine was then switched on, and CI Burns said his name, time and date. He included the name of the WPC in attendance, and then mentioned why Mary McCaferty was being questioned. He said that they were making enquiries into the murder of a Frank Muir.

"Mary McCaferty, I know you knew Frank Muir at one time, is this why you went to see him in Spain?"

Mary is shocked that they knew about her trip, so she hesitated before replying. "Who told you I was in Spain."

However, the reply from CI Alec shocked her even more.

"We were informed about a murder victim by the name of John Williams, alias Frank Muir, who had had an affair with a blond haired woman, who we heard had been dating an Alan Deans. Alan had fallen out with Frank Muir and had murdered him over this woman. Now why did you go there, wear a blond wig and mess things up between the two?"

Mary's mind is now in a spin, she is so surprised

at these questions, and does not know what to say to him.

"Perhaps I should have a lawyer attend, before I say any more."

CI Burns talks into his recorder and says that Mary McCaferty has requested a lawyer, and he is ending the conversation. Then he switches the recorder off. He tells her that she will be held in a cell until her lawyer could attend.

Mary is fuming now, "I cannot stay here," she shouts, "I have customers to attend to, back at my work, you have to let me go."

"I am sorry Ms McCaferty, you have to remain here until I finish with my questions, and we will inform the hairdressers that you will be unavailable for the rest of the day."

Mary is led to a cell, and while there, she is asking herself questions, where is my Ian, why is he not here to help me, what exactly do they know?

I have to really think before I say any more.

Mary's lawyer arrived forty-five minutes later, and he was shown directly to her cell. Another forty-five minutes passed before they were ready for CI Burns again.

Back in the interview room, the tape recorder was started again. The name of the lawyer was added to the recording and questions resumed after the introductions.

The CI was soon asking her why she had messed about with both men,

"My client has no comment," said her lawyer.

"Why did you go to Spain Mary?"
Again, the lawyer answers,
 "My client just fancied seeing the place after hearing about it from your Detective Inspector Ewing."
 CI Burns continues,
 "However, you knew that Frank was there, so why did you have sex with Alan Deans?"
The lawyer told him that his client could have sex with who ever she wanted to, whenever she wanted to; it was of no business of his.
 "Why did you tell the hotel that you were going to Torrevieja for a week?"
 Mary's Lawyer said,
"My client had been scared that Alan would chase after her after she had jilted him, so she said that to put him off the trail.
"You knew that Alan Deans was going after Frank, so why did you not call the Guardia?"
 "She was terrified, and ran away as soon as she could," said the lawyer.
 "Why did you tell DI Ewing that you were going to Ireland, when in fact you knew all the time you were going to Spain?"
 Mary replied this time, "yes, I did know I was going to Spain, but I thought that if I told Ian, he would try to stop me."
 "By saying Ian, I presume you meant Detective Inspector Ian Ewing."
 "Yes I did", Mary, replied.
 "What is your relationship with DI Ewing?"
 "No comment," said the lawyer; "my client regards

that as a private matter, if you want to find out, you should ask him yourself."

"Did you have sex with DI Ewing Mary?"

The lawyer then said to him that he was beginning to get too personal and it had nothing to do with a murder in Spain. Unless he was going to arrest his client, they would like to leave.

A very red-faced DI Ian Ewing is sitting behind the mirror.

"Before you go Mary, Another question, what happened to the blond wig?"

"You can answer that one," her lawyer said to her, as he already knew what she was going to say.

"I was taking it of at Almeria airport before going through customs, and a woman sitting next to me admired it. I asked her if she would like to buy it, and we agreed on a very reasonable price. I have no idea where she was going, so sorry chief Inspector Burns; I cannot tell you what happened to it after that. It could be anywhere in the world by now.

The Chief Inspector sighed, and then said,

"Did you kill Frank Muir?"

My client does not need to answer that question and as I said, we would like too leave now.

CI Alec Burns knew he could not hold her any longer; he spoke into the recorder and said the time, and that the questions were finished.

The machine was switched off and reluctantly agreed to let them go.

Mary's lawyer told him that he would take Mary back to Dingwall with him, so she would not require the police transport.

CI Burns said thank you, you are free to go meantime.

On the drive back to Dingwall, her lawyer told Mary that she had done well and that the police should not bother her again. Mary thanked him and asked to be dropped off at the hairdressers where she worked. He said that it would be no problem, and it was fine by him as his office was near by.

Back in the police office, CI Burns says,

"Well Ian, with the knowledge that the skeleton at Barrylairg was John Williams, not Frank Muir, at least we have closure on our Barrylairg skeleton case. We know that Frank and Alan were responsible for murdering John Williams, and with Alan Deans spending a long time in a Spanish jail, as far as The Guardia in Spain is concerned, they have closure on their murder case."

He goes on to say,

"How Mary McCaferty is involved, we will never know for sure Ian. Even who was it that killed Frank Muir? Was it Mary or Alan? It is funny to think that the Barrylairg mystery is now solved, but the Mojacar mystery remains, however you have done a wonderful job Ian, and I think that you had a great time doing it."

Mary's boss was pleased to see her back and was soon asking why she had been taken to the police station. She told her it was all about a murder in

Spain, and it turned out to be an ex boyfriend of hers.

"He had been abducted in 2014, and it was believed back then that he had been murdered. It turned out that he had arranged the whole thing, so that he could disappear to Spain. He had made enemies of some drugs people and he was scared for his life." Mary continued with a little lie.

"The police think that the drugs people may have caught up with him, and they wondered if I knew anything about them. Of course I did not, so they told me to go home."

"Well thank God you were not involved Mary, I would not have been able to keep employing you if you had been. You better pop off home love; it must have been a bit stressful for you, I will see you tomorrow."

Mary thanked her and headed home.

Mary is now back in her flat and wondering why Ian had not been in touch, she was a wee bit upset with him. She was asking herself, should I call him or not, no, bugger him, if he could not help me when I needed him, Ian Ewing, you can go to hell.

/ ## CHAPTER 31

Friday July 12th. 2019.

Mary has just left the hairdressers where she works, and as she is walking near to the Bank of Scotland, she is suddenly aware that next to her, two masked people had jumped out of a van and one held a gun to Mary's head, and the other was shouting at a man carrying a small case. He was saying to him to get on his knees and shut up or the woman gets shot.

Mary turned and looked straight into her assailant's eyes and noticed that it was a woman, and she looked shocked.

Next thing Mary knew was that she was struck on the side of her head with a glancing blow from the gun, and she fell to the ground. When the ambulance arrived, she was semi conscious and after being checked out, she was taken to Ross Memorial Hospital in Dingwall.

After she had been treated at the hospital Doctor Bell, who was attending Mary, told her that she had received three stitches in the wound on the side of her head and as she was still a bit groggy, they would be keeping her overnight.

A nine, nine, nine, call comes into the local Police station at Bridaig Ave. where PC Brian Smith immediately passes the message through to his superior, at the main police station on Burnett Road, Inverness. He informs Detective Inspector Ian Ewing that an emergency call had come through from the Bank of Scotland, on High Street, in Dingwall. He said the call informed him that an armed attack by two masked robbers had taken place outside the bank premises, and there were reports of injuries. He informed the DI that Dingwall police were already at the scene.

Detective Inspector Ian Ewing knocks on the door of Chief Inspector Alec Burns office, he enters on the command, "come in, oh its you Ian! What have you got for me today pal?"
Ian says to his CI,
"An armed robbery has taken place at the Bank of Scotland in Dingwall a few moments ago, and at least one customer has been injured. Our people and the ambulance services are there now sir."
The CI says,
"I take it you have put the normal stop points into operation Ian?"
"Yes sir, all main roads out of Dingwall will be covered within the next few minutes."
"Okay Ian, let's go," said the Chief Inspector.
On the way to Dingwall, they are discussing,

could it is possibly connected to the robberies in the Central Scotland area earlier this Month.

In Dingwall the Chief Inspectors car is passed through the cordoned off area and the Sergeant in charge brings him up to date about the attack.

He says,

"At the same time as the man carrying the case was being attacked, a female was passing right next to him in the opposite direction. The woman was also stopped and a gun was held to her head. The one with the cutting tool shouted to the man with the case to get on his knees and shut up, or the woman gets shot. As the case was being cut free, the assailant with the gun, smashed it into the side of the woman's head, and she had fallen to the ground with blood pouring from the wound. As she was semi conscious, the ambulance crew decided to take her in for treatment. She is on her way to the Ross Memorial Hospital as we speak sir."

DI Ewing asked if there is a name for the injured woman, the Sergeant tells him that her name is Mary McCaferty, from the hairdressers shop next door.

CI Burns and DI Ewing turn and look at each other at the same time, CI Burns says to his DI,

"Bloody hell Ian, I think you better head over there right away, take my car, I will get a lift back to the station by a Constable."

"Thanks sir," came the reply.

Detective Inspector Ian Ewing arrives at the Ross

Memorial, where he is shown to a waiting area and is informed that a Doctor Bell would come and talk to him. After fifteen minutes the Doctor comes over, he introduces himself, and explains to DI Ewing that his patient is doing well considering the blow she had received during the attack, and that she had received three stitches in the wound.

The doctor said that he had asked Ms McCaferty if she was okay for a visitor, and she said that she was not feeling like it just now. However, when I told her that it was a DI Ewing that was here waiting to question her, she seemed to perk up quite a bit. Therefore, you may go in to see her, but please, only for a few minutes.

"Certainly Doctor Bell, I do understand," said DI Ewing.

As he entered the ward, Mary turned her head with a slight groan but with a big smile, she said,

"It is great to see you again Ian."

"Likewise," he told her, and Ian had a big smile on his face as well. The two had shared an evening together at Mary's apartment, a few months back, and Ian had not forgotten what happened that night.

"What puzzles me Mary is why they attacked you, it had not happened on previous robberies, which we suspect that the pair had been involved in?"

Her reply was one that surprised Ian. She told him that the one with the gun was a woman.

"What, this is very important Mary, it could be crucial to us in catching these two, because they had masks on, are you sure it was a woman?"

"Yes Ian, I am positive, the woman knew that I had recognised that fact because I could see that she had fear in her eyes. She was obviously very frightened. I think that is why she hit me."

When Ian asked her how she was so certain, Mary explained that she could see the false eyelashes, and she had on the same perfume that she, Mary, used herself.

"Wow Mary this is amazing, but I am really sorry that this has happened to you, how are you feeling?"

She tells him that she is very tired and her head is sore, "but it is so nice to see you Ian, I have missed you."

He asks if Gerry, her brother is coming up to see her, but she says that he will be in a wheel chair for the rest of his life and it was too long a journey for him to sit in a bus from Dunfermline to here.

At that point, Doctor Bell comes in with a nurse and says to DI Ian Ewing that he must leave now as his patient needs to rest. Ian agrees but says,

"Just one more question, did you notice the colour of her eyes?"

Mary replies, "Yes I did Ian, they were dark brown."

DI Ian Ewing thanks Mary, and kisses her on her cheek, on the good side of her face. He says to her that she has done a fantastic job, and her information would be conveyed to CI Burns and sent down to Strathclyde police as well.

"I will be back to see you tomorrow again Mary."

"I will look forward to that Ian, love you."

Doctor Bell looks at the nurse and they both smile, DI Ewing says goodbye, and as he leaves the room, with a slight blush on his face. The nurse looks at Doctor Bell and whispers,

"There must be at least twenty years between those two, and I do not think they are father and daughter, I wonder what is going on there?"

The next day, back in his office at Inverness Police HQ. DI Ian Ewing is saying to Alec, his CI, that he is going back to the hospital this morning to check on Mary McCaferty.

"That's fine Ian; see if she can remember anything at all, ask her if the woman possibly said something, or even what kind of footwear she had on, every little bit of information helps."

Ian tells him he will and says,

"See you later Alec."

Ian is on the way to the Ross Memorial Hospital in Dingwall, and his mind is not just on the case, but Mary McCaferty as well. He just cannot get her out of his mind, even though he knows that she had somehow been at least an instigator to a murder in Almeria, Spain. He keeps trying to convince himself that Mary must have been an innocent participant in what had happened in Mojacar.

Mary knew otherwise, but she would never let on to anyone that she had been the person who had wielded the murder weapon. With what he had arranged to be done to Gerry, her brother, Frank Muir, had deserved all he got, and so did his accomplice Alan Deans.

On arrival at the hospital, DI Ewing enters the ward and receives a huge smile from Mary, who says, "hello Ian I'm really pleased to see you today, I have great news from the doctor, he says that I can go home today."

Ian replies and tells her that he was happy to hear that, "when are you allowed to leave?"

She says that she could go home as soon as the Doctor had been on his rounds, which is normally just before lunchtime.

"Well that should be within the next hour," says Ian, "and I guess that you need transport Mary?"

"Yes Ian and I was hoping that you could help me with that," she says to him, with that beautiful smile of hers.

He told her that it would be his pleasure to drive her home, and possibly help her if she required any groceries on the way there.

"That would be wonderful Ian, but I will need to go home first to check, I cannot remember what I have at home."

Ian tells her that he would be glad to pick up a few things for her if she needed them.

While they waited on the doctor to come round, the two sat and chatted about how strange it was that they had an attraction for each other, especially with the age difference, Ian said that it was easy for him as she was such a beautiful woman. Mary smiled at him and said,

"Thank you Ian that is a very nice thing to say, but it was also easy for me as you are such a gentleman."

Just then, the doctor arrived and said, "Well Ms McCaferty by the sound of you, you have certainly got well very quickly, I guess your friend here has really cheered you up."

Mary's reply brought a slight look of surprise from both the Doctor and DI Ewing.

"Ian is my boyfriend Doctor, and yes every time I see him, I feel wonderful. I am ready to go home now and he is here to take me, so can I go?" Doctor Bell gave her a quick check over and told her that she looked very good considering the fact that she had been hit on the side of her head with a metal object.

"Yes, Ms McCaferty your boyfriend can take you home now; just take things easy for the next few weeks."

"Okay Doc I will, just as long as I have my Ian to help me I will be fine."

Doctor Bell says with a little smile.

"Good bye and good luck to you both."
Ian picks up Mary's handbag that had been brought in by the ambulance crew, and said to her,

"Okay let me get you home Mary."

On the way, back to Mary's apartment Ian says to her that not only the Doctor, but he also was a wee bit surprised when she said that he was her boy-friend. Mary laughed and told him that as far a she was concerned he was, she had never met a man as nice as him, and that she wanted to be his girl friend.

"How about it Ian, are you up for having a much younger woman to love you?"

He was surprised by the suddenness of her state-ment, and was not quite sure what to say.

"I, I do not know what to tell you Mary, I suppose that you know I really like you, but there is about twenty two years between us, what would people think?"

Mary again shocked him by saying,
"I do not give a fuck what people think Ian; all I know is that I love you. Oops, I am sorry for the bad language, but it is how I feel about you, I love you Ian."

"I need time to think Mary, I still wonder as to why a beautiful young woman would want to be with me."

"How many times do I need to tell you Ian, I love you, and that is all that matters to me, not your age, please be my boyfriend?"

By now Ian is starting to come to think harder on how he could cope with a younger woman, he knows that he is somehow attracted to her in a strange way, is that love he is thinking to himself, I do not know, it has been so long.

"Okay Mary I will agree to meet with you a few times to see how we get along."

With that, Mary grabs at him to give him a big kiss, and nearly makes him loose control of the car. Luckily, there was no other traffic on that part of the road at that point.

"For Gods sake Mary be careful, we could have crashed there."

"I am so sorry darling, I am just so happy."

They arrive at Mary's apartment and Ian helps her out of the car and takes her hand to help steady her into the building and then into the lift to her door. They enter and he tells her to sit down while he checks to see if she needs any groceries. He returns from the kitchen and says that the bread she has is stale so he will go and get some,

"How about I bring a take-away back with me Mary?"

She asks him if he could get a Chinese and that he would get the money for it in her purse.

"Bugger off Mary, my treat; I am glad that you are feeling good. I will also get some fresh milk when I am out; I suspect that the one in your fridge could be off by now."

Mary said, "thank you darling." She was one very happy woman.

By the time Ian arrived back at the apartment, he noticed that Mary had her dressing gown on, and had two glasses of wine on the table with candles placed in the centre. The curtains were now closed, and the main light had been turned down low. Ian sensed the warm atmosphere in the room, and his eyes were draw to the gorgeous woman who was standing there smiling at him.

He placed the food on the table and took the bread and milk into the kitchen, after he had placed the milk in the fridge, he returned to the living room to find that Mary had the Chinese food all set out on the table. Ian walked over to her and kissed her on the forehead; he then pulled out her chair and as she sat down, he pushed it in behind her.

Mary said, "thank you darling, can I dish out your food for you?"

"No thank you Mary I will help myself, I do not eat a lot of food and I have to look after my figure."

After they had finished eating, Ian rose to clear the table, but Mary said to leave it, she would clear it in the morning. "It will give me something to do, please come and sit on the sofa with me."

During the conversation, Ian asks her if she had remembered anything more about the woman attacker.

"As a matter of fact, yes I do," she said, "when I landed on the ground, I noticed under the trousers she had on, she wore a kind of black shoe. Not the usual kind of shoe a woman would wear for every day use, but more like the type that policewomen wear."

"Are you sure about this Mary?" asked Ian. "This could be very important lass."

She told him that she was positive because she would never be seen dead in bloody heavy shoes like that. They both laughed.

Ian continued the conversation by saying that

this could be very important to the case.

"At least something good has come from the injury that you received Mary, not that I am happy about it."

She said, "Its okay Ian, I know what you mean. Now let us change the subject."

During the small talk that followed, Mary asked him to stay the night with her, but Ian told her that he still had to report to his boss, especially as he had her latest information to pass on.

"It could be the lead we need to catch these buggers, and if we do, you will be in for a large reward Mary."

Mary was a bit disappointed when he refused to stay, but then the thought of a large reward cheered her up a bit. Wow I could be rich, she is thinking.

She said to him,

"I meant what I said Ian, I love you so much, and I want to spend the rest of my life with you. If you need to take it easy with our relationship, then I will accept that, not entirely happy about it, but as long as I have you near me a lot, then I will be patient."

"Thank you," he said, "I do need to make sure I am doing the right thing, I have feelings for you that I cannot explain, so please bear with me."
She butted in by saying, "That's what I would love to do at the moment Ian, be bare with you, but in my bed."

They both laughed, and Ian said to her that she was still ill and needed more rest.

"We will talk about our relationship in a few days, however I do need to get back to the office and report in."

As Ian was putting on his jacket to leave, Mary took the opportunity to grab him round the waist and give him a long and sensuous kiss. Then she said, "Don't be too long in coming back my dear."

As he left, he told her that he would see her very soon.

It is Thursday afternoon and DI Ian is calling on 'his girlfriend' Mary McCaferty in Dingwall.

"Mary if I showed you a picture of the woman that hit you with a gun, could you recognise her?"

She said, "By seeing those eyes in a picture, it would be very likely, but if you could put a fragrance to that picture, I am certain I could. Why Ian, what has that got to do with this case?"

He said to her, "the police in Perth have a female suspect that worked for the police and that they would love to have you identify her."

Mary agreed to help and it was arranged that Ian would take her to Perth.

Monday twenty second July, and Mary got the call from DI Ian Ewing, to pack an overnight case, she became very excited, at last she thought, a night away with the love of her life. Up until now, they had never spent a whole night together. The fact that it was her thirty-ninth birthday; she was intent on making it a very good night, Mary promised herself that she would give Ian a night that he would not forget in a long time.

When Ian had booked the hotel in Perth, he had been in two minds, one room or two. Bugger he thought, it is her birthday so I am going for it, one room for Mr. and Mrs. Ewing please.

On the drive south, Ian was saying to her that he hoped she would be able to pick out the suspect.

"Do not worry my dear," she replied, "I am certain that I will. So you believe that this woman, who hit me during the theft, is involved with a Glasgow drugs syndicate as well Ian?"

"Sorry Mary I am not wanting to talk about the case, however if I am right, this ID will go a long way into helping catch the people who attacked you."

It is seven pm and they are just entering the outskirts of Perth,

"Soon be at the hotel Mary, and I hope you do not mind but I have booked us into the same room as husband and wife."

When she heard that, Mary was about to give him a huge hug but remembered that he was driving.
She told him that she was delighted and that he would get the big hug in bed that night.

On entering the hotel, and as usual, the difference in age is always noticed. The receptionist gave them that enquiring look that said, you two are here for a dirty night together, but she said nothing other than welcome to Perth Mr. and Mrs. Ewing, your room is on the second floor. There is a lift at the end of the hall. I hope you have a nice stay.

Ian took the key from her, said his thanks, then took Mary's case and headed for the lift saying, this way dear. Mary gave the receptionist a look that said. I know what you are thinking bitch, and it is none of your fucking business.

After they had settled in, they left the hotel for a walk around to find a nice place to eat.

During the meal, she was telling him that she had been so looking forward to spending a full night with him at last. Ian's face went a little flushed and he told her that he was a little nervous. He then produced a small box and handed it to Mary, and wished her a happy birthday.

"Wow Ian I did not know you knew it was my birthday," to which he replied,

"I am not a Detective Inspector for nothing." Mary opened the box and took out a lovely necklace, and after asking Ian to help her put it on, she said,

"I also have a little surprise for you, and I am sure that you will enjoy this evening."

"What are you up to Mary?" but all she said was that he would have to wait and see.

On the walk back to the hotel Ian was still asking her what she had as a surprise, but Mary just laughed and told him that all will be revealed.

Back in the room, Mary told Ian that she was

going to the bathroom, so you had better be in bed by the time I come out darling.

"I am looking forward to it Mary." He replied.

When she came out of the bathroom, Ian was already in bed and wearing his PJs. She wore the tiniest black and red nightdress that came down just far enough to reveal the small bush between her thighs. She had shaved the letter 'I' in it and said to him,

"This is your surprise dear; I had this done just for you."

Ian was amazed at this almost naked beauty standing in front of him, then he saw that she was pointing to her pubic hairs, he noticed his initial very neatly trimmed in her bush. His face went so red that he tried to hide under the covers, but when she pulled them back, she burst out laughing.

"Right you bugger, you are getting them PJs off now."

When he was completely naked, Mary climbed on top of him and began her teasing, beginning with kissing him on the neck then his nipples. She made sure the letter I of her bush was rubbing gently on Ian's penis. He was enjoying the teasing with what this beautiful woman was doing to him, and at the same time he was imagining the letter I, that was rubbing against him. There was no doubt that Detective Inspector Ian Ewing was having a night he would never forget

Next morning after they had both showered they made their way to Perth Police HQ, in Ian's car. Before they entered, Ian told her to act as if they were not a couple. If they thought that, it may alter the way DI Grant looks at your decision, so be very careful Mary, no holding hands.

Mary was a little excited with the fact that she was helping to catch a criminal; it would never be made known that she had been one herself. She would take that secret to her grave. Even the love of her life, Detective Inspector Ian Ewing would never be told the truth of what happened that day in Spain.

She was thinking, I have no regrets, that bastard Frank deserved all he got. Suddenly she was brought back into the present world; Ian is asking her if she is okay,

"You looked miles away for a few seconds there Mary."

"Yes, yes Ian, I am fine, I am a wee bit nervous in case I fail to recognise the woman."

He told her not to worry,

"I am sure you will be able to pick her out."

They were taken to a room and had to wait for Chief Inspector Graham Liddell to enter. When he did, DI Grant introduced them to him.

The police in Perth had a number of pictures for Mary to look at and she was then asked to look and study each picture carefully. After she had, she identified two pictures as her assailant.

Ian was taken aback by this action from his witness, he is thinking, what is she doing, she had said that she was certain that she could pick out the right one.

Chief Inspector Graham Liddell then said,

"Well-done Ms McCaferty. We tried to trick you with the extra picture; yes, it is the same woman but with her hair photo shopped to change her appearance."

He turned to DI Ewing and congratulated him and his witness; he went on to say,

"This has brought us a huge step forward in the case."

DI Ewing without thinking said to them,

"You bastards, you might have told me what you were up to."

Both the CI and DI started laughing and told him that they had already been told that he and Ms McCaferty had been seeing each other lately, and they did not want any conflict with their relationship, and with her choice from the pictures.

CI Liddell thanked them both for coming all the way down to Perth and he hoped that they would have a safe trip back to Dingwall.

When they were on their way back up the A9 to Inverness, then on to Dingwall, Ian says to Mary that she had almost given him a heart attack when she produced two pictures. She laughed and said I saw it in your face Ian and I am sorry if I upset you, do not worry darling I will make it up to you later.

Ian smiled and told her, later will have to wait for a few days Mary, last night was special and I need a few days rest. She laughed and told him that she did not want to stress him out so she would take care.

Ian took her straight home and told her that he would need to report to his boss CI Burns and let him know how successful a trip it had been, Mary spoke up by saying,

"Successful in more ways than one my dear, are you coming back here tonight?"

His reply was,

"No, I have a few things to sort out at home."

She was quick to say,

"I could stay at yours darling."

Ian told her that he still needed time to sort his mind out, however if she thought that he was taking advantage of her he would understand.

Mary started to cry, I am so sorry Ian, I love you and I do not want to lose you. Whatever you want to do is fine by me, if you just want me part time I am happy, as long as I still have you. Ian was sad that he had upset her, and said to her that he was possibly feeling, he was falling in love with her, but he just wanted to make sure. This brought a smile to Mary and she said,

"That is the best news I have ever heard. Whenever you are ready Ian, I will be here for you."

As Ian was driving away from her apartment, he was questioning himself, 'is this what you really want Ian, I could go back to the life I was living pre

Mary McCaferty, or I could say to hell with it and go for a life with her. '

What he did not realise was that, what Mary really wanted was a relationship with a man who would treat her well, not just a bed mate, and that she would have a safe and secure life. Mary had never had that security or any financial stability all her life, and Ian Ewing could give her all that.

Now back in Inverness, CI Alec Burns is asking DI Ewing what the latest news is.

He says, "Emma Gibson turned out to be the person who had attacked Mary with a gun during the robbery in Dingwall, Mary had identified her. Perth had informed me that the others in the group of robbers were her husband George, and a Bill and Sandra Cummings. George, Bill and Sandra had suffered terrible injuries at the hands of the Glasgow drug cartel, who they had also robbed at one time.

George Gibson and Sandra Cummings had both died, but Bill Cummings had survived with serious injuries, and Emma had escaped with no injuries, she was now on her own and had disappeared to Spain."

Alec says, "Unfortunately, Emma Gibson is possibly going to get away with it, unless she decides to return to Scotland and tell the police all that she knows. At least we have helped to put an end to the robberies here in Scotland Ian, and by the way pal, how is your girl friend, you not proposed yet?"

"Mary is doing well and thanks for asking, but no, I have not asked her to marry me."

Grant was heckling Ian.

"About time you did pal, you are not getting any younger; take her away on holiday and come back married."

Ian said as he left the office, "Bugger off Alec,"

Alec said "bye Ian and mind that holiday."

That evening Ian Ewing is headed from his home in Inverness, to Dingwall. He had invited Mary out to the local Hotel for dinner, and when he saw her, he was pleasantly surprised. She had decided to wear a blonde wig for the evening; he told her it changed her looks completely. Mary of course knew that it would as she had worn one similar when she had been in Spain.

After dinner as they relaxed in the hotel lounge, Ian told her that he had been talking to CI Burns earlier. He had said to thank you for helping with the bag snatch robbery and then joked about us both going on holiday. Mary said,

"That is a fantastic idea Ian, Why not, where would you like to go?"

"Really Mary, I was only joking when I said it."

"Ah well Ian, I think we should and you liked Spain didn't you?" He told her that he had never been abroad before he had been for that week in Spain earlier in the year.

He said, "I suppose it would be nice to go back for a proper holiday."

"Right my dear leave it to me," she said, "I will book

us into a nice apartment, so that we can have a lot of private time together. I have had a wonderful evening Ian so now you can take me home for a cuddle on my sofa."

Next morning after Ian has left for work, Mary is searching her laptop for a suitable apartment in the Mojacar area. She thought about her experience there on her last visit, so she started looking further along the coast. This was when she sees a beautiful beachfront apartment in a place called Vera Playa.

She checked for flights to Spain and then managed to get the apartment booked for the suitable dates.

She then calls Ian to tell him that their holiday was booked and they were going in four days time.

"I have booked us a very nice beachfront apartment Ian, so we can sit on the balcony and enjoy the sea view."

"Blooming heck Mary that is quick, you certainly did not mess about arranging it, and how long are we away for love, because I had better tell my boss as soon as possible."

When Ian told CI Burns, he replied,

"I have told you for ages now Ian, it is about time you had a holiday, go and enjoy it, and mind the postcard. Hmm, it's not a honeymoon is it?"

Ian replied, as he walked out of the CI's office laughing.

"No it bloody well is not, and for that remark, you can stick your postcard sir."

CHAPTER 32

Almeria Airport.

When the flight arrives on time from Glasgow, it is early evening. After entering the arrivals area, Ian and Mary collect their luggage, walk through the customs, and head for the car hire desk. It took them an hour and ten minutes to drive to Vera Playa, where they were to meet someone who would take them to the Apartment they had rented.

As both walked into it, they were amazed at how nice it was. The woman explained a few details to them and said, because their arrival was late at night; a small groceries basket had been set up for them. It contained tea, sugar, milk, bread, butter, jam and biscuits.

They thanked her for her help and told her that they would be in touch if they needed anything.

As Ian carried their cases into the bedroom, Mary headed into the open area kitchen and put a kettle on for a cup of tea, and then both sat out on the decent sized balcony. While they drank their tea, they looked out onto the beautiful Mediterranean

Sea view.

After the long day traveling, Ian suggested they to go to bed when their tea was finished. Mary did not argue she could hardly wait to get into bed with him.

The next morning when Ian got up, he was in for a big surprise. As he walked out onto the balcony and looked down on the beach, he was amazed at what he saw, there were a few people walking on the sand, and they were completely naked.

He immediately went back in to tell Mary, who had just come out of the shower.

"There are naked people out there Mary."

With that, she laughed and told him,

"Oh I forgot to tell you darling, I booked us into a naturist resort, and that is what people do here."

Ian told her. "Aye well you can forget that, if you think that I am going about naked you can think again."

"Do not be a spoil sport dear, if I can do it, so can you."

"What! You mean you are going to strip naked and walk out there in front of other people, no way."

She gave him a big smile and removed the towel that was wrapped around her, and told him,

"You do not have to if that is your wish dear, but I am proud of my body and I will go naked out there along with every one else here."

Ian agreed that she did have a beautiful body but did not know if he could get used to her parading it in front of other people.

"Well first thing dear, is that I need to get dressed, and then have a cup of tea and a bit of toast before we go shopping. I noticed last night that there was a map on the little desk, of where the shops and restaurant/bars are. Therefore, we will talk about our little differences later."

After the groceries were bought and returned to the apartment, they sat on the balcony and talked about each other's thoughts about going naked. Ian told her that he had never even dreamed about stripping of and walking about in public. Mary said that she had never done it before, but had always wanted to try it, and this was a fine opportunity.

"Maybe we could have lunch in that bar down on the beach and see how things go dear."

"What you mean people actually go into bars naked?" he said.

"Yes but they must always have a towel round them when they are inside eating. Do not worry dear; I will be holding your hand to comfort you."

"Aye well Mary, if a naked man sits down next to me, I am going to run away as fast as I can."

She laughed at him.

Before they went out for lunch, Mary changed into a long loose fitting sarong, but did not tell Ian that she was naked underneath it.

They decided to go to the restaurant she had seen right next to the beach, and they sat inside to eat lunch. After which they then went outside with their drinks and sat at a table on the edge of the beach to look at the view.

Ian was surprised at how many people were clothed; he had thought that everybody would be naked. Mary told him that as she knew they were coming here, she had been reading about naturist places and every one was like this. Go dressed or go naked, but if you are dressed then you are likely to be the odd one out.

"What would you do dear if I stripped of now and had a little walk on the beach."

"Huh, I bet you wouldn't dare," he said.

No sooner had the words come out of his mouth, Mary pulled the sarong up over her head, and as she walked out onto the beach, she said,

"You just lost your bet darling."

Ian was so shocked he was lost for words. She shouted back to him,

"Are you not coming with me dear?"

He just sat there and shook his head. Ten minutes later, she walked back to their table, pulled on her sarong, sat down, and just smiled to him.
He said,
"Mary, you really took me by surprise that time you bugger."

"I loved it dear, it gives you a great sense of freedom, and I am going to come back and do it again; however, next time you are going to walk with me, even if you have to wear clothes.

"We will see he replied," They enjoyed another gin and tonic each then left to go back to the apartment. When they got there, Ian took hold of her sarong, lifted it over her head and led her straight to the bedroom. He told her that he had got quite excited at the sight of her naked body when she was walking back towards him. Well obviously, you still are excited my dear, when she saw his erection as she helped him strip off.

Saturday morning, after a late breakfast the couple prepared for the beach again, Ian in T-shirt and shorts, and Mary with a different sarong and nothing else. With the attention that Ian was paying to her, she did not hide the fact that there was nothing underneath this time.

As the apartment contained beach chairs, they took two and a sun umbrella with them, along with a book each.

While Ian sat reading, Mary took her sarong off and lay naked on a towel next to him soaking up the sun.

Ian's reading was not going too well, as he kept looking at the naked beauty lying next to him.

After a while, another woman, who was on her own, walked close by them and settled down naked on a towel. Ian quietly said to Mary,

"Please sit up a minute dear I have something to tell you."

She said, "Oh are you going to go naked after all dear."

No listen, I have to say this quietly, but you see that woman lying just over there, she is the spitting image of the woman you pointed out in that

ID picture back in Perth. You don't think that it could possibly be her do you?"

"Christ Ian, really, anyway how come you noticed what her face looked like, or was she not naked when she passed."

You are not funny dear but yes, she does look like that woman, but how can we find out, I just cannot walk right over there and ask her."

"Well you can't dear but I can, watch me."

Mary rose and walked down to the waters edge, had a little paddle and then walked up towards the place where the woman was lying. Right away, she recognised that she was the person who had hit her on the side of her the face, with a gun barrel.

Without a second thought, Mary was standing next to her and said, "Well hello Emma, imagine seeing you here."

Emma sat up in shock, and she started to say,

"Should I know you," then she stopped herself and said, "I think you have the wrong person, my name is not Emma."

"Yes it is Emma, and I do know you, don't you remember hitting me in the face back in Dingwall."

As her face reddened she replied, "I, I am sorry but I think you are wrong, whoever you are."

"No I am not wrong Emma, it is you and I want to talk to you."

Emma started to get up but Mary told here to stay where she was or she would call on a police officer to come over. Mary told her too move over a bit on the towel, so she could sit down. Emma was so taken aback; she did as she was told. Then Mary started to tell her, that her boyfriend was a police inspector and that he was in charge of the robbery in Dingwall, and that she knew everything that had happened.

"Listen Emma," she said, "I am not here to cause you concern, in fact it is completely the opposite.

For a start, my name is Mary and I completely forgive you for the incident. I know you were very frightened; I could see it in your eyes. Anyway, if it had not happened I may never have met Ian, and I am so in love with him. I have you to thank for that."

Emma was now very confused but said, "I am sorry for hitting you Mary, and I do not know what else to say to you, other than, I am happy that you have met the man of your dreams. How ever did you manage to find me?"

She explained to Emma that it was pure co-incidence and that it was Ian who had recognised her as she had walked past him. Emma asked where he was, and Mary told her that he was the shy man sitting back there with his clothes on.

She went on to ask Emma if she could wrap her towel around herself, and go with her to talk to him, she said that Ian would be less embarrassed if she did that. They both had a little laugh and they both stood, then Emma wrapped the towel round her body.

When they reached Ian, Emma was surprised to see the age difference between the two, but she did not mention it. Mary pulled on her sarong after introducing Emma to him.

After a couple of minutes Ian suggested that they all go back to the apartment he and Mary had rented, and they could sit out on the balcony and chat better. Emma told them that she would need to go back to her place to get something to wear, but Mary told her that she would let her have a loan of one of her sarongs. This was agreed and all three left the beach.

During the meeting, everything was explained to Emma about her friend Bill Cummings, and that he had survived the attack also that he was very keen to see her again.

Ian suggested that if the two of them could get together and return the stolen money, then both would most likely, not receive a prison sentence.

Bill has remained in the hospital as it turns out to be his only option. He told the police that after what had taken place there, he would never ever go back into their apartment again.

Ian went on to explain that her husband George, and Sandra Cummings could not have a decent funeral until she returned to Perth and arrange things with Bill.

Emma told them that there was no way they could return the funds from all four of the robberies, especially after Bill and Sandra had lost their entire share.

Ian explained to her that the robbery in Glasgow would not come into the equation as it had never been reported, so after talking to Bill Cummings and he agreed, they would only have to return the money from the other three.

"I believe that the total from those robberies was one hundred and fifteen thousand Pounds. If Bill could clear part of this from the sale of his apartment, and Emma we know that you must have a fair bit of your share left, so could you manage to raise the rest of the funds."

She asked, "Do you really think that we will not have to go to prison Ian? If that were the case, I would not hesitate in going back. George and I did buy an apartment here but there is sufficient funds left to cover the balance. Wow, could you confirm that for me?"

"No Emma, I cannot confirm it, however I can have a word with my boss in Inverness, and ask him if he could talk to the relevant authorities. So if they could do that, then I take it you will promise to return to Scotland."

"Yes most definitely Ian, I promise, however what happens if I return to my home, and someone comes after me?"

"You will now be perfectly safe to return home. If you agree to the police instructions Emma, I will contact my chief Inspector. If he can get confirmation, by Monday, and if you can get on the same flight as we are on, then I will tell him that I will personally escort you home."

"Yes, please do that, I have been so alone here, it will be nice to see Bill and take care of the funerals.

I will be able to tell him that he can stay at my apartment."

Mary suggested that Emma could stay with her if it would help. However, Ian told her that if the insurance companies drop their charges by getting their money back, and the fact that Mary had retracted her charges. The court may take into account that they have both lost their respective partners; there is a good chance that both Bill and Emma would have a house arrest device attached to their ankle.

Emma said to Mary that she could never thank her enough for what she is doing.

"You are one very special woman Mary."
She told her.

"Thank you Emma but as far as I am concerned, I have a very special man in Ian Ewing."
The afternoon had gone well and Ian explained that his boss would probably get back to him on Monday. He said that he was hopeful and all should be well.

When it was time for Emma to head back to her own apartment Ian joked with her.

"I hope you are not going to do a runner on us Emma."

"No way Ian, this is my one and only chance to put things right, or as right as they could be. I am so happy for both of you to be here and help me."

CHAPTER 33

Ian surprises Mary.

On Sunday morning, Mary said that she wanted to spend more time on the beach, so the beach chairs came out again, and as soon as the temperature warmed up, Ian was sitting in his chair on the Playa trying to read a book, while Mary lay down naked and enjoyed the sun. After about an hour and a half, she stood up and told Ian that she was going for a walk.

"I'll be back in fifteen to twenty minutes love."

Ian watched her walk away, and he is thinking that he should be with her, but he looks so out of place with a pair of shorts on, however nobody pays any attention to the naked body's walking about.

Go for it Ian, he said to himself, no I can't, yes I can, no way.... Bugger it, he slipped off his shorts and pants and walked in the direction that Mary had gone. She had walked about two hundred meters when she decided to turn and go back, imagine her surprise when she saw a completely naked Ian walking towards her.

"Wow, Ian, is that really you?" She ran towards him and gave him the biggest hug ever.

"You went naked at last."

As he walks hand in hand with Mary, back to the beach chairs. She tells him that he had just made her day by surprising her like that."

"Oh I am full of surprises my dear," he said.

That evening Ian and Mary went out to another restaurant that had been recommended by another couple of guests of the apartment complex they were in.

After the wonderful meal, they sat enjoying a glass of wine each and Ian said that he had had a wonderful time here in Spain, "However," he said,

"I still think that Florida would be a much better place to go for a honeymoon Mary."

To begin with, the suggestion did not seem to sink in to Mary, as she replied,

"Yes Ian it probably would be a nice place to go, I have often wished to go there sometime, but never been able too."

Ian smiled and said again, "Yes I do think that it would be a nice place to go for a honeymoon Mary," and he looked at her with a do you realise what I am saying to you expression on his face.

She noticed the strange look and thought to herself, why does he keep going on about a nice place for a honeymoon, and then it dawns on her,

"Fucking hell Ian, are you asking me to marry

you? Oops, sorry for swearing darling, but were you asking me to marry you?"

He laughed and said, "Yes Mary, I really am asking you to marry me, Will you?"

"Of course I will you silly bugger, I would be most happy too. In fact, I am so happy I could cry. I can't wait to tell Emma tomorrow, can I call her now?"

"Not now Mary, I want this to be a very special evening, just the two of us."

She replied, "You better believe it my dear, I will make it even more special when we get back to the apartment."

Mary kept her promise.

The next evening, as they had accepted Emma's invite to dinner, Mary told Ian to get the bottle of white wine out of the fridge, to take with them. They both then walked the two streets to her apartment.

On their arrival, Emma welcomed them with a hug each, and said that she had a gin bottle on ice ready for them. They sat on her second floor balcony and chatted for a while, subject being, how Emma and her friends had got into the robberies, in the first place. It was a long story and after an hour, Emma suggested that they go in for dinner. They could continue the conversation later.

After dinner, they returned to the balcony for Emma to continue her story. Ian listened with great interest as to how Sandra had planned each and every robbery.

He said, "Although she had been very meticulous with her plans, what with Emma's eyes and her shoes being noticed by Mary, it just goes to show how the least little thing could give the game away."

Emma said, "Yes, we had thought that we had got away with it all, that is until Mary had came on the scene. I know it is too late now, but I wish we had never done it. I have lost George and Bill has lost Sandra all because we got greedy."

Before Ian and Mary left that night, it was certain that she and Emma had hit it off, and were becoming good friends. Emma said.

"See you both sometime tomorrow."

After they left, Ian said to Mary,

"I hope we are doing the right thing here, I would hate for it to backfire on us."

Return to Scotland,
Wednesday, Eighth September

As the flight arrives very late in Glasgow, Ian had pre booked two rooms in the hotel at the airport.

He had arranged for his car to be delivered there early next morning, by the company that had looked after it for the last week.

On the drive north, Emma wondered if she should be dropped off at her own place, in Perth, but Mary said, "No way, you and I will go to Perth together on Friday when Ian goes back to work.

That way I can be there to comfort you if you need it, which I reckon you will."

They all arrived in Dingwall about one pm, so they had lunch at a local restaurant before Ian took the women to Mary's home. He then kissed Emma on the cheek and Mary on her lips, and told them he would contact them in the morning.

Before he headed to his cottage, he went straight to police headquarters in Inverness to bring Chief Inspector Alec Burns up to date with everything.

Well almost everything, he did leave out the beach time he had enjoyed there. The CI was not too surprised to hear that his DI had become engaged, all he could tell him was that he was a lucky man, and wished them both all his best wishes.

Ian asked if Bill Cummings had been informed of Emma's return and he was told, "Yes he has, and he is so excited about seeing her again. He has also been told that he could move into Emma Gibson's flat as soon as it could be arranged. He had been happy at that suggestion, and hoped that Emma could assist him with clearing his apartment, as he did not want to go into it again.

CHAPTER 34

News from Spain.

Detective Ian Ewing decided that he would eventually put his cottage up for sale as there were too many memories of good times with his late wife. He had thought that he would not be settled there with Mary. When he did sell it, he would move in with her until they found another home.

Once they were married, they would buy a nice home in Dingwall, that way Mary would be able to continue her work for as long as she wanted. Ian had begun to contemplate retirement.

Perth, Two months later

Bill had used the spare room for about five weeks, before he and Emma decided that as they had both been in her bed before, he should just as well be back in it now. He had also sold his apartment, and with Emma's funds, they cleared off their debt to the insurance companies.

When they had both appeared in court, the judge had sentenced them each to two years in prison, Bill and Emma looked at each other with horror.

However, the judge had stated that as they had

returned all the reported stolen money, and in addition, Ms McCaferty had dropped the assault charge. The fact that they had both lost their respective partners he reduced the charges to two years suspended sentence. The ankle bracelets were removed and they were free to leave.

Emma and Bill had decided to sell her apartment in Glebe Park, Craigie, and head to Spain to spend the rest of their lives there. With the proceeds from that, and the money that Emma still had in a bank in Spain, they would have a hundred and fifty thousand Euros in savings. Along with that, they would be living in Emma's apartment that she and George had paid for in full, so life would be perfect.

Emma had called Mary to tell her what they were going to do and that she and Ian would be more than welcome to stay with them if they went back to Spain on holiday. Mary and Ian wished them well, and told them that they might one day.

By November 5, the sale of Emma's apartment had gone through, and their next move was to transfer the funds to Emma's bank in Spain, that way they would not have to worry about carrying a large amount with them as they travelled.

Next, they packed their car with all the necessary things that they would need to start their new life there. They planned to drive to Plymouth, where they would sail to Santander, in Spain. As the ship takes twenty hours fifteen minutes for the overnight journey, they would be able to have a sleep, which would break the long trip.

The drive south went well, and they boarded the ship on November 12.

It is now Wednesday thirteenth of November and soon after arriving in Santander, they had cleared customs and were looking forward to the drive to Vera Playa, Almeria.

The journey would take them about nine and half hours, so they set off immediately.

DI Ewing's desk phone rings, and he gets a message to go and see CI Alec Burns. Who says, as Ian enters his office, "Hello pal, have a seat, I have some news for you. I just received a message from Perth police, who had a report from passport control. I have to tell you that there had been a very bad auto accident near Torrelavega, in north Spain.

I am sorry to be the bearer of bad news Ian. Emma Gibson and Bill Cummings were involved in the accident and both had died at the scene. They had only travelled in Spain for half an hour when it happened, I am so sorry Ian. I think you had better take the rest of the day off, and go tell Mary."

"Thank you Alec, I will." Ian said.

When Mary received the news she was devastated, she cried on Ian's shoulder for a few minutes. She eventually said, "I can't believe it Ian, I was so hoping to go and spend some time in Spain with them."

Ian continued to console her. "Please stay the night with me?" She asked him.

"Yes Mary I will." he replied.

CHAPTER 35

Monday November 18.

The news came through from the insurance companies involved in the robberies. Because they had received all of the stolen money from all the robberies that Emma and her friends were involved in, they had decided to pay the reward to the person responsible for the return of their money.

That person is Mary McCaferty, and she was to receive the sum of eleven thousand five hundred and fifty pounds. This was ten percent of the stolen money, from each of the three companies involved. The hand-over was to take place at the local police station in Dingwall, and the local press was present for the presentation of the cheques.

Mary was so surprised at the amount, as she had never had that sum of money all her life.

One month later, she was to receive another surprise. A letter arrived at her apartment, from the Attorney dealing with the estate of Bill Cummings and Emma Gibson. When Mary contacted the company in Perth, the attorney told her that she had to come to Perth, so that they could go over the will in private.

The appointment was made for Friday, December 20.

It was a cold and frosty morning as Ian and Mary were driving down the A9 to Perth. She was wondering how she would cope with the reading of a will from her best friends. Would she feel as cold as the weather was outside the car?

Soon they reached Perth, and eventually found the Attorney's office. After finding a place to park their car, they had a three-minute walk to the address.

When they entered the Attorney's office, they were shown through to the boardroom, and soon a woman appeared and thanked them for coming. She asked who it was that was with her, and Mary explained that it was her fiancé.

After checking Mary's identification details, including her passport, the woman told them that she was the Attorney, and then went on to explain the details of the will.

The Attorney told Mary that they had received a sum of money from the Spanish bank, and after conversion, it came to one hundred and twenty eight thousand, eight hundred and fifty pounds.

Mary just sat there with her mouth wide open, and she turned to Ian, who was almost as much surprised as she was. She asked the Attorney to repeat that last statement then said,

"Are you certain that she has left that to me?"

The Attorney explained, as there was no family involved, she was the only recipient on the will. All Mary had to do was to give the Attorney her bank account number, and after they had taken their costs from the will, they would transfer all the remainder to her account. The funds would be in her account within twenty-four hours

She went on to explain that she had also been left the deeds to an apartment in the Very Playa area, in Almeria, Spain. The Attorney handed the Spanish apartment deeds to Mary, who told the Attorney that she would call her first thing on Monday morning with her bank details.

The drive back up the A9 was a quiet one, with it being so silent, Ian thinking that Mary was still trying to take it all in.

All of a sudden, she was now a very well off young woman with a home in Spain.

At the same time Mary McCaferty was thinking, wow I am now rich, and have a new home in Spain, waiting for me. Now what could I do with all that money? I could just give notice on my rental apartment in Dingwall and head off to Spain.

What she was not thinking about, was the loss of her friends who died in the vehicle accident, and the fact that she would be walking away from her finance, Ian Ewing. The man she had promised to spend the rest of her life with.

After arriving in Dingwall Ian suggested that he take her for dinner to celebrate her good fortune, and Mary was delighted to accept.

During dinner, Ian asked her how she felt, and she told him that it still had not sunk in.

"Give me a few days to take it in," she said.

Ian usually stayed the weekends with Mary and they always made love several times, but this time she was being extra enthusiastic during their sex.

Over the weekend, Ian never brought up the subject of her inheritance and she never mentioned either.

Mary's mind was in constant turmoil

"Is money more important than love?"

DI Ian Ewing was back at work on the Monday, when he received a message from his solicitor saying that he had a couple wanting to view his cottage on Tuesday about four pm. This was good news for Ian as it had been on sale for at least a couple of months, and he had had only one other viewing.

He called Mary to tell her his good news, but as she was unavailable. He left a message to say that he would call round to see her after the viewing, and let her know how it went. When she called back, the answer he received was a strange one, "I might not be in when you arrive, but I hope you are okay, love you."

On Tuesday, and after the couple had viewed his cottage, they had said that they would probably be putting an offer in within the next day or two.

As he was driving over to Dingwall to tell Mary,

he was thinking that he would soon be living with her full time.

On arrival at Mary's address, he parked his car and took the lift to her apartment. As he had a key, he did not bother to knock on the door. Imagine his surprise when he noticed that there was a strange appearance in the place. He then noticed a note on the table in the centre of the living room, it said.

I am so sorry my love, but I have decided that I need to move on. If you have sold your home, you can continue with the rental of this place. I have left a message for the property owner to let him know.

Lots of love,

Mary. xxx

Mary McCaferty had chosen money over love.

Ian Ewing was shocked after he had read the letter from Mary, but he knew he had to get over her. He had always thought that there was something in that mind of hers that he could not work out.

He knew that she would have probably gone to Spain, but he did not want to follow her. He cancelled the sale of his cottage and did what he had done when his wife had died almost twenty years previously.

DI Ian Ewing set his mind on his work for the Scottish police, with thoughts of retiring in the near future.

Once more, he would be alone at Christmas time.

CHAPTER 36

Mary is pregnant.

In Spain, Mary McCaferty is living the life that she had never dreamed she could possibly have had, and she had lots of male attention.

In the two months that she had lived there, she had already tested out three males. The first, a Spanish waiter caught her eye, but he was very possessive and did not like the way other men looked at Mary.

Juan said to Mary that she should not be alone in a bar at night when he had to work; it was not the Spanish way he told her. Mary told him to go and fuck himself in the Spanish way, because she was finished with him.

Next male friend was a Swedish man; however, it was only a one-week romance as far as she was concerned, especially after she found out that he was already married.

Her third male friend was an Englishman who owned a bar in Turre, a town not too far from Vera Playa. Gazza was a typical Londoner, very noisy and full of himself. He expected Mary to help him out in his bar on the nights that it was very busy; however, he never offered to pay her.

Nevertheless, he did expect her to stay the night with him. Mary soon tired of him using her as slave labour and his mistress.

Even though Mary had enjoyed sex with those men, it was never as good as she had had with Ian Ewing.

Ian knew what a woman wanted from sex and he had never disappointed her. Yes, older men were better sex partners; however, the older ones here were not to her liking, they all seemed to have fat bellies.

Mary had plenty money in the bank, but at thirty-nine years of age, how long would it last without an income. Especially when she knew she was pregnant.

She thought to herself, even though she knew who the father was would he be interested. I doubt it.

What to do about her condition, should she get an abortion, should she have the baby and get it adopted or should she keep it.

She eventually made up her mind to keep the child and bring it up on her own; she knew that younger men would not be chasing a pregnant woman, so she decided no more sex. Mary also decided not to try to contact the father; he would probably just deny he was.

Because of her upbringing, Mary knew she had the ability to take care of a child and herself.

February 2020.

Mary had heard of a Covid virus that had begun in China and it was spreading fast throughout the world, and by the end of January lockdowns were being considered in various countries.

She is now thinking that she would possibly be better off having her baby in Scotland, so she called Gerry, her brother, and asked if she could move in with him. She knew that he stayed in a two-bed apartment in Dunfermline, Fife, and that he would have room for her.

Gerry was happy to hear from his sister and about the news that she was pregnant; he said he was looking forward to being an uncle. He did ask Mary who the father was, and when she told him, he said to her that maybe she should contact him first and possibly, he may want you to stay with him.

"No I do not want that Gerry, I am sure he would deny he was the father, I want to come back to stay with you."

"Okay Mary, because of this Covid, there is word of a lockdown coming to Scotland soon, so the quicker you get here the better."

Mary booked her flight for the next week and then began to stack all her personal things in a large cupboard and fitted a padlock on it. Next, she set about arranging for an apartment rental company to look after her place, as the rent would be a nice earner for her.

As expected Covid 19 hit hard and the UK was soon into lockdown. Mary was pleased that she had taken the decision to return to Scotland.

Gerry lived in Abbey Road, Dunfermline, it was a flat, in a three-story building and the address was 1c. He had been offered this one as it was on the ground floor, even though he did not require two bedrooms this had been the only one available at the time Gerry became disabled. Now the two bedrooms were becoming very useful. There were no more men friends in Mary's life.

The months passed by, and when August came along Mary gave birth to a healthy seven and a half pound boy, who she named Sean, after her father.

Unlike Mary, Sean had light brown hair and she was sure she could see a likeness to his father. During the rest of 2020 and 2021, because of the lock down, Mary looked after Gerry and Sean, and only left the house when she had to.

2022 and the winter had passed, Sean was now sixteen months old, he was getting up to all the things that boys of that age get up too.

The worst of the Pandemic had passed and it was so much easier to get around, so Mary decided that maybe she should look for a job. Gerry would be on hand to look after Sean so there was no reason why she could not work.

She called Hannah, her old boss in Dingwall, and

asked her if she could write a reference letter for her. Hanna was happy to hear from Mary and told her that she would do so no problem, she said,

"Anyway Mary, lets hear all your news and what you have been up to lately."

After hearing that Mary now had a son but no husband, Hanna also said to her that she should come up to Dingwall so that she could see her son and that they could stay at her house for a couple of nights.

Mary thought that it would be nice and they agreed on a week on the Friday. First, though she had to check out a car hire company, as she did not own a car, then she set about arranging for the trip.

A thought came into her mind; maybe she should take a trip into Inverness and visit her old flame Ian Ewing, and then she changed her mind. She knew that she must have hurt him so much when she had left him the way she did.
Best give him a miss she said to herself.

The route to Dingwall would take her from Dunfermline, up the M90 to Perth, then north on the A9 to Inverness, where she would continue on the by pass around the city. Then over the Kessock Bridge for the final part of the journey to Dingwall. 220 km drive would take her about two hours fifty minutes, and as the A9 section was one of the most notorious stretches of roads in the country she was hoping that the weather would be favorable for her.

Nine thirty, Friday 11 February saw Mary load

a large suitcase into the boot of her hire car, and then safely strap young Sean into a safety seat behind the passenger seat, as he would be happier there with being able to see her.

The drive up the A9 went well and she was thanking her lucky stars that there had been no problems or accidents to cope with.

From the Kessock Bridge, she had dual carriageway up as far as the village of Tore; from the roundabout there, she would take the A835 and be in Dingwall in less than fifteen minutes.

Mary was following behind a bus and saw it signaling to pull into the bus lay by for Kilcoy Castle, she was thinking, good I have a clear run into Dingwall now.

Unfortunately for her, a truck driver had not noticed her car that was behind the bus, and he pulled out right into Mary's lane. There was no time for her to avoid the accident and her car crashed under the rear of the truck.

The vehicle that had been traveling behind Mary had managed to stop, and the passenger, who was a nurse, told her husband to call the emergency services while she goes to check the car.

As she approached it, above the hissing of escaping steam, she could hear a child crying.

A quick look at the driver told her that the female was seriously injured, and then she checked on the kid in the back. She could see that it was a small boy and he had a few cuts from the flying glass from the windshield. Sheila, the nurse, unfastened the crying child from the seat and handed him to her husband, then did her best to see to the driver who was unconscious.

Within minutes, fire services, police and two ambulances arrived. It was clear that the driver would need to be cut free from her car, which would take some time.

A Sergeant Brand from Dingwall police was talking to Sheila and her husband, who still had the little boy with them. They were giving him their statements and telling the Sergeant that the female in the car had no chance of avoiding the truck.

Sheila's husband, whose name was John, said that the truck driver, should not have come out of the junction as his view was obviously restricted with the bus.

The Sergeant thanked them both and asked Sheila if she could take care of the child until the medics took over. Sheila told him that she would go with the boy in one of the ambulances as she was on her way to work in the Ross Memorial hospital anyway.

Sergeant Brand again thanked her and said that a DI from Inverness would probably want to talk to her later, Sheila said, "Okay with me Sergeant."

At Police headquarters in Bridaig Avenue, Inverness, Chief Inspector Alec Burns had just received the information of the accident.

Within fifteen minutes, he was attending at the scene just as Mary was being released from her vehicle. After talking to Sergeant Brand, he had a quick chat with Sheila just before the ambulance left with her and Sean in it.

With the vehicle being a hire one, it would take time to find out who the victim is, so he asked Sheila if she knew.

As she could not reach the drivers handbag, which was on the floor of the passenger side, Sheila had no idea of names for the victims.

CI Burns thanked her and said that he would get a Constable to check with the rescue crew to retrieve the handbag. He would then let the hospital know the details. As the rear doors of the ambulance were being closed, Sheila thanked him.

A member of the fire rescue crew had picked up her handbag and handed it to PC Jones, who took it to his CI. When Alec opened it, he checked for the identification of the driver. That was when he got a big shock; Mary McCaferty was a name that he was very familiar with, and so was his now retired Detective Inspector Ian Ewing.

The medics told the CI that the driver was still alive but in a very poor condition, they hoped that she would make it to the hospital.

Alec also checks in the woman's handbag to see if there was a name for the child, that name also shocked him.

CI Burns knew that it would be up to him to inform Ian of the accident, but first he would attend the Ross Memorial to check up on Mary.

The news he received was that Mary was in a coma and they would keep him up to date when, and if, the victim came round. CI Burns thanked them. He then asked if he could talk with the nurse who brought the child in. Alec was directed to the ward where she was working, and he was pleased to see that Sheila was still taking care of Sean.

He explained briefly to Sheila what he knew of the family and asked her to keep that information to herself until he got back to her. Sheila said that she was glad to help and that she would personally care for the boy.

CHAPTER 37

Sad news for Ian Ewing.

Ex Detective Inspector Ian Ewing was surprised to see the visitor at his front door and asked him,

"What brings you here today Alec?"

Alec Burns told him that perhaps if he would ask him in then he would explain.

"Firstly, Ian I have to tell you about a serious accident that I attended earlier today. There was a female driver and a small boy in a child seat in the back of the car. The female injured in the accident was your old lady friend Mary."

"What! But she is in Spain Alec, it can't be her."

"Yes it is her Ian, and the rest of the news is that the child is called Sean Ewing."

"Bloody hell Alec, I don't know what to say to you, a child with my name, it can't be?"

"Well Ian that is what is on the identification we found in her bag, so that is all that we have to go on. Mary was still in a coma when I left so I did not get a chance to talk to her, but just before I got here, the hospital messaged me to say that she had come round. I suggest that you get to the hospital as soon as you can Ian and find out for yourself. Would you like me to come with you pal?"

"No thanks Alec, this is something I have to do on my own, but thanks anyway."

Although Mary had dumped Ian Ewing after she had come into money, he still had feelings for her. What those feelings were he was not quite sure of, however they were there, so he had to go to the hospital to see her.

There was also the question of the little boy, Sean, if it was his, why did she not let him know. Was she scared to tell me, was she thinking that I would deny it was mine, or maybe it is not mine but she gave it my name? Possibly that could be the reason she left me as she did.

These questions were going through his mind as he drove to the Ross Memorial.

When Ian arrived at the hospital he was directed to the room where Mary was, however he was informed that she had been sedated and was fast asleep. He told the nurse that he would head to the canteen for a cup of tea and come back later, but if she did come around to call him ASAP.

The nurse said that she would but continued to tell him that Sean was in another ward, and being looked after by a nurse Sheila, perhaps you should go see him first.

Ian walked to the ward and stopped outside the door. He is saying to himself, do I really want to do this. Suddenly the door opened and a nurse asked him why he was there. Ian told the nurse, who had said that her name was Sheila, that he was here to see Sean Ewing, "My name is Ian Ewing." He said.

Sheila asked if he was the boys grandfather and she was surprised to hear him say, "No, but he might be my son."

Sheila said, "Sean is very stressed, so please be patient with him. He keeps asking for his mum, so we told him that she was sleeping and we did not want to waken her, it's a lie I know but in a way, she is sleeping."

Ian said that he would take care.

His instant thoughts were when he looked at Sean, who appeared to be asleep, was bloody hell that could be me. He just stood there looking at the lad and wondering what to do next and turning to Sheila, he asked her what was to happen with Sean? She replied that they had found out that Sean's mother had a brother in Dunfermline called Gerry, and he had been called. We did not know about a father.

Gerry it turns out is in a wheelchair and finding it difficult to arrange to come up to Inverness.

Ian asked for Gerry's telephone number and said that he would arrange that for him. Just then, his phone rang and the caller told him that Mary had come round again and would like to see him. Ian took a long look at Sean and headed back to see Mary.

Before he entered her room, a nurse spoke to him and informed him that Mary had received a serious head wound along with a broken ankle and a bad cut to her knee. Ian thanked her for the information and then as he entered the room, he smiled to Mary and said that he was pleased to see her. Mary replied,

"And to see you my love, then she broke into tears and kept repeating, I'm sorry, I'm sorry, I'm so so sorry Ian. What have I done to you?"

Ian took her hand and told her that there was nothing to be sorry about, he had understood. Then he leaned forward and kissed her.

"Have you seen Sean," she asked, "he's your double Ian, I'm sorry I left you, I'm sorry I never told you, I should have come back home but I was so frightened that you would tell me where to go. He is definitely your son Ian, that I know for sure, please look after him for me."

"You can do that yourself when you get better Mary, and you both can live with me. I am going to contact Gerry and see if I can arrange for him to come to Inverness to see you."

"Wow that would be really nice Ian, I was wondering how he could get here. I don't know if he can afford a hotel, but tell him to put it on my account."

"No Mary, he will be staying with me, and that way we can look after Sean until you get home."

Mary again burst into tears and said,

"I loved you Ian, I really did, it was the money that I was thinking about, I had never had so much all my life. I was so stupid to leave you."
"Well now you are back and we can all live together

here in Inverness. You just have to get better first."

"But I remember you saying that you would not like me moving into your cottage, it had so many memories of your wife."

"Things are different now Mary, Heather was always sorry that she could not give me the son that I wanted, I am sure she would be happy for me to have you and Sean, my son, staying in the home she loved. You will enjoy living there Mary."

"I will try Ian, I will try, I'm so sorry."

Doctor Bell came into the room and as soon as he saw Ian, he said, "it's nice to see you again but I'm sorry it is under such circumstances."

He remembered Ian when Mary had been attacked during the robbery in Dingwall.

He continued to say, "Mary needed to have a head scan as they suspected that there could be some brain damage. If she has hemorrhaged, he would have to operate right away. She would then require a lot of rest. As she is now awake I would like to do the scan now. Perhaps you can come back tomorrow as she will need rest and sleep after the scan."

Mary tried to argue with him but Ian calmed her down by saying that he would be back first thing in the morning.

"It is getting late now Mary so I best be going to try and contact Gerry for you."

He gave her another kiss and told her that he would be back to see her first thing in the morning. Before he left the hospital, he did think about going to see Sean again, and then changed his mind, better not in case I upset him he thought.

As soon as he got home, he called Gerry, who told Ian that he was feeling very sad, as he could not get up to Inverness to see Mary. Straight away Ian told him that he was arranging the journey for him.

He was to get a train to Inverkeithing and change there for Inverness; Ian continued by telling him that he was paying for the trip, and he, Gerry, would be staying with him while he was there.

"I can't do that Ian,"

"I'm not doing it for you Gerry; I am doing this for Mary and Sean, so get yourself sorted out and on that train tomorrow morning. I will be at Inverness station to pick you up, from there I will take you to my home, and then we will go see Mary."

Gerry thanked Ian and told him that he really appreciated what he was doing, he continued,

"I will see you tomorrow."

Saturday morning saw Ian at Ross Memorial, before he entered Mary's room he saw the duty nurse who told him the Mary had had an operation on her scull to release the pressure on her brain. She said that the op had gone well and Mary was feeling better this morning. Just be patient with her as her speech is a bit blurred. "I will he replied."

He received a big smile from Mary when he went in, but her "hello dear" came out as 'lo der'.

Ian smiled and told her that Gerry was on his way to Inverness to see her and that he would be here tonight. A tear came from her eyes as she tried to speak,

"Thak you dalin, I am lookin forard to seen him." Although it also came out sounding like a foreign language, and Ian smiled when she had replied. However, soon her eyes closed and she fell asleep.

Ian walked down to the hospital canteen for a cup of tea before heading back up to sit with Mary. He stayed there until it was time to go to the station to collect Gerry at five o'clock. At half past four, he kissed Mary and told her he had to go but he would be back later with Gerry. Again, he received Mary's best smile.

Ian collected Gerry at the station, and after loading his wheelchair into the boot, they headed for his cottage on the west side of Inverness.

After which they drove to the hospital and firstly went in to see Sean. They met Nurse Sheila and had a talk with her about Sean.

Because Sean was perfectly well, it was agreed that they could take him home with them tonight, they would collect him when they came back from seeing his mother. Sheila said she would be sorry to see him go but she was happy for him. She would arrange to have everything ready for them. Sean burst into tears when he saw Gerry, and ran as best he could into his arms, crying, "Uncky Gerry, Uncky Gerry."

Ian stood back and gave them a few minutes together before Gerry had the chance to introduced Ian to Sean as his daddy. Sean was not quite sure of him at first, he had been told that his father was working in another country and could not get home. Gerry assured Sean that this was his dad and encouraged him to give him a great big hug.

Ian felt a strange sensation as Sean did this and a little tear appeared in an eye. It was his first tear since the loss of Heather just over twenty years ago.

He told Sean that he, and Uncle Gerry were going to see his mummy, and then they would come back to take him home. Sean cried and said that he wanted to see his mummy, but Gerry hugged him and said that he would have to wait until tomorrow. This seemed to satisfy Sean, who said,

"Ok, cos I want to go home. Mummy told me we were going to stay in another house."

Ian told him that he would be staying in a lovely new home tonight, and because he had been so brave, he would have his own room. Sean was now very excited at the thought of having his own room, now he had his mind on that rather than seeing his mum. At that point, Ian and Gerry took the opportunity to leave him and go see Mary.

Seeing them both come into the room Mary burst into tears, there were no words coming from her, she was just so happy.

After lots of hugs and kisses, the talk led to Gerry being lucky to stay with Ian so that he could be close to her. Mary looked at Ian and tried to say thank you, and he interrupted by saying that Gerry could stay as long as he wanted.

Doctor Bell entered the room and asked to see Ian privately, so he made his excuses and left the room.

"Okay Ian, I have to tell you that Ms McCaferty was hemorrhaging and the blood was putting a lot of pressure on her brain." He explained, "I am hoping that she will get better, and with her ankle in plaster, she may be able to go home in a week or so, however, the head injury may get worse Ian, and if it does, there is not much we can do for her."

After Ian asked what her chances were Doctor Bell told him, about fifty fifty.

Ian said that he understood and that he would explain to her brother later. The doctor thanked him and reminded him that it would be best if they did not stay too long as his patient required a lot of rest.

It was about an hour later and the two left a now sleeping Mary to go and collect Sean.

After they arrived at Ian's cottage Sean was excited to see his room, so Ian took him through to a bedroom at the rear of the home. Ian was surprised at the excitement from Sean, what he did not realise was that he had always slept in the same room as his mum. This was an adventure for him.

Ian told him that he would get him something to eat and then if he wanted he could get into his new bed. Sean said, "Yes please dad."

Ian could not hold back the tears when he heard those words.

Later after Sean was in bed and sleeping, Ian

and Gerry were chatting about his and Mary's past lives. He is beginning to realise why Mary had done what she had when she came into a huge amount of money. She had never had the comfort of being financially secure.

Ian then began to explain to Gerry what the doctor told him about his sister's injuries.

"What am I going to do Ian, if she is not able to look after herself; there is no way that I can. I only have two bedrooms and it would be difficult to look after her and Sean."

This was when Ian told him that he had an idea.

"What if you move here to Inverness permanently Gerry, and stay here, you could help me look after Sean and Mary. Once she gets home, I want her to sleep in my room, so you can stay in the room you are in tonight, and with Sean having his own room, it would be a perfect solution."

Gerry was surprised at the offer from Ian and said that there was no need to do that, he would manage somehow, they always had.

Ian told him that he was not taking no for an answer, it was settled as far as he was concerned.

"Let's drink to it, do you want a beer or a whisky Gerry?"

Sunday morning and all three set off for the hospital.

Mary had had a comfortable night and she was sitting up a little bit when they entered the room. Sean, who had been sitting on Gerry's knee in the wheelchair, saw his mum, and he wanted to run towards her. Ian lowered him down and watched as his son ran to his mum, shouting,

"Mummy, mummy, mummy."
Ian had to lift Sean up onto the side of Mary's bed, but told him to be careful. He could hardly wait to tell his mum that he had his own bedroom, and said,

"Can we stay there forever mum, please can we?"
Before Mary could reply, Ian said,

"Of course you can son, and so will Uncle Gerry."
Mary gave Ian a questioning look, which said, what was that all about.

He explained to her that Gerry was going to move to Inverness and stay with them.

"By them, I mean you, me, and Sean." More tears from Mary.

The morning went so fast and eventually Mary became very tired. Her visitors said that they would go for lunch and would come back in the afternoon to see her. Sean wanted to stay with his mum, but Gerry told him no and that was enough, Sean slid down off his mum's bed and said ok. With that sorted, Mary smiled and said,

"See you later," which sounded more like
'She oo aterr'.
When the afternoon visiting time came, Gerry moved his wheelchair back from the bed a little to let Ian sit next to Mary and hold her hand, and again Sean was on the bed.

The afternoon passed quickly and it was time to

head home, the hugs and kisses went all round and Sean again wanted to stay, but the look from his uncle was enough to say no.

Ian suggested a visit to McDonalds on the way home and that was it.

Five fifteen Monday morning Ian's phone rang, it was the hospital. Doctor Bell here Mr. Ewing,

"I have to inform you that Ms McCaferty had not had a good night. She had been complaining that her head was sore, we gave her medication to relieve the pain but we are very concerned about her condition. Can you come in immediately?"

"I will be there right away Doctor."

Ian knocked on Gerry's door and when he heard, come in, Ian explained about the phone call from the hospital.

"Get yourself there now Ian, I will look after Sean, please let me know how she is as soon as you can."

"I will Gerry, thanks."

Ian contacted the doctor as soon as he got to the hospital, and he escorted Ian to the emergency room that Mary had been taken too. Mary was semi conscious when they entered and she smiled to Ian and said, "Hello darling."

It was said as perfect as it could be which surprised Ian. He held her hand and kissed her, and said, "I love you Mary."

Mary replied, I love you too Ian." She closed her eyes and was gone.

Doctor Bell walked up to Ian and said,

"So sorry Mr. Ewing."

Ian did not hear those words; he had just lost the love of his life for the second time.

Once he got home, he had too explain to Gerry and Sean that Mary had passed away.
"You must stay here now Gerry, I will need you to help me look after Sean."
Gerry said that he would be happy to stay.

Reviews for
Time on my hands

Autobiography of a Master Clockmaker

5.0 out of five stars, Adventures and accidents!

Reviewed in the United Kingdom on July 20, 2020

A tale of life's highs, lows and downright bloody-mindedness. Dreams that almost turned into nightmares, however, Jack and Sheila's love and support for each other, plus their sheer determination...they have made it work. Long may their happiness in Spain continue. Maybe with a few less mishaps though.

Diane.

5.0 out of five starts, Enjoyable read.

Reviewed in the United Kingdom on 15 August 2020
I enjoyed this book, having known Jack for a few years and I am able to say he is a genuine nice guy, it was interesting to read of his experiences growing up and becoming a Master Clock Maker.

David.

ABOUT THE AUTHOR

Jack Anderson.

Born 2nd. November 1945.

At the age of fifteen, Jack left school and began
an apprenticeship as a master clock maker.
He opened his first business in his home town
of Ladybank, Fife Scotland, in 1974

Jack married Sheila in 1967 and the couple
had two children, Kevin and Carol

By 2001 their children were grow
up and the couple had decided to
emigrate to Florida, USA.
There, they eventually began their own
business. In 2017, as Jack had gone through a
major cancer operation 3 years previously, and
with 46 years dedicated to his craft, the couple
decided to retire,
They sold their successful business in Naples,
Florida, and moved to Partaloa, Spain.
He was bored during the Covid lockdown
so, Jack began writing his autobiography.